Grange Hill Rules – OK?

Matters were going from bad to worse towards the end of term at Grange Hill, especially for Tucker Jenkins. Here he was, for instance, being given a last warning by the Head: 'Grange Hill and you do not suit one another at the moment. One has to change.' Any more trouble and Tucker would be for the chop, a prospect that delighted eavesdropper Doyle. But even when Tucker tried to toe the line, things didn't go right. He thought Penny's fund-raising plan of a sponsored walk was a big yawn and suggested instead a sponsored silence. But Trisha countered with a sponsored slurp-in and everything slid from the sublime to the ridiculous. What started as a positive move by the kids to stop guerilla warfare with Brookdale was now leading them straight for disaster in their own camp.

ROBERT LEESON

Grange Hill Rules-OK?

Based on the BBC television series
GRANGE HILL
by Phil Redmond

FONTANA · LIONS

First published in Fontana Lions 1980
by William Collins Sons & Co Ltd
14 St James's Place, London SW1
Second Impression February 1980
Third Impression March 1980

Printed in Great Britain by
William Collins Sons & Co Ltd, Glasgow

Chapter 1

0700 hours on a cold December morning and the Magnificent Seven of Grange Hill were still wrapped in their blanket rolls.

No! One was awake. Little Benny Green had his clothes on and was creeping downstairs. Mum left for work twenty minutes ago. Dad had been up half the night with his back, but now was asleep at last. Benny had found a way of earning some much needed pocket money. But he was keeping it to himself for the moment.

As he reached the main road, heading for the shops, he passed a parked car. The man at the wheel took careful note of him as he went by.

0800 hours. Penny Templeton Lewis chewed toast and marmalade as she went over her notes for the Year Assembly that morning. The School Council had decided on a big charity sponsored walk – in competition with Brookdale School. For the tenth time, Penny wondered what they'd all say when she put the idea to them. Peter Jenkins would object – naturally. If there was one thing he hated more than walking, it was organized walking. Trisha Yates would object, too. Just lately everything Penny said or did seemed to get right up Trisha's nose. Penny shrugged and stuffed her notes into her bag.

Twenty minutes later, she was in the car, passing through the shopping centre on the way to school. Suddenly her mother braked and swung the car to the kerb.

'Look, there's that sweet little Justin Bennett. Let's give him a lift.'

Penny grimaced. Justin was all right, but, well . . . She knew they'd sit there and say nothing to each other all the way to school, while her mother made bright conversation.

Anyway, she didn't want company right now. Then she noticed that Justin had a carrier bag and was dodging into the supermarket.

'That's funny,' said her mother. 'I wonder why they do their shopping down here?'

She started the engine again and Penny relaxed.

Justin hurried out of the supermarket, checking the things in his carrier and the money in his hand as he ran. He dived down a passage at the side of the building, sprinted across a car park, into a narrow entry between two old tenement blocks and turned along the pavement of a street where half the houses were demolished or falling down. Stopping by an old, three-storey house, he climbed up the stone steps to the front door, fiddled in the letter box, and fished out a key on a string.

Across the street, a man in a parked car put his notebook away in his pocket, let in the clutch and drove slowly away.

08.45 hours. Trisha Yates and Cathy Hargreaves strolled along the pavement of the main street heading towards school. Trisha chatted idly about this and that, but she had a suspicion that Cathy wasn't really listening.

'Year Assembly first thing today,' she said to Cathy.

'M-mm.'

'Wonder what old Tumbledown Lewis is going to put on us today?'

'It's Templeton Lewis.'

'That's what she says. What d'you think?'

'About what?'

'About what I'm talking about!'

6

'What's that?'

Trisha rolled her eyes. 'Where are you? You haven't heard a thing I said.'

Cathy didn't answer. She was thinking about Neil. She didn't know his second name. He had grey eyes, with flecks of green, and curly eyelashes. They'd met in the shopping centre on Saturday and she was meeting him (she hoped) again this afternoon. She wasn't telling though, because he went to Brookdale.

As Trisha and Cathy were walking along to school, Peter Jenkins (alias Tucker) was struggling out of bed. He'd had a bad dream last night. Mr Llewellyn, the Headmaster, had called him in and said: 'Your last chance, Jenkins. One more stupid, irresponsible or deliberate act of disruption from you before the end of term and I shall call in your parents. Grange Hill and you do not suit one another at the moment. One has to change. You have fifteen days left to work out which one it shall be.'

As Tucker struggled into his clothes he remembered. It wasn't a dream. It was true.

He splashed cold water on his face, slipped into the kitchen, trapped a stray piece of bacon between two rounds of bread, and reached the road, half-knotted tie flying, bag trailing, while his mother was still calling 'Peter, hurry up.' No sign of his mate Benny. No time to call for him. That was a right start to the day. At the stop he was carried on to the bus in the midst of a scrum of Grange Hillites. He ignored them all.

'Hey, Tucker, struck dumb?'

'Getaway. He's taken a vow of silence. Like those old monks.'

'What, the ones with filthy habits?'

'Very funny,' snarled Tucker.

'Hey, it's alive.'

7

He barged his way off the bus and caught up with Benny Green and big Alan Humphries by the zebra crossing near the school gates.

'Hey, look,' said Benny, pointing to the other side of the road. 'That car was down the shops this morning. Now he's here. What d'you reckon he's after?'

'Flasher,' suggested Alan.

'What, in a car?'

'S'right. That's why they have those automatic roll down windows.'

'You made that up.'

'I know, it came to me in a flash.'

At 08.30 hours there was still one in bed. Michael Doyle. His father, chairman of the School Governors, no less, was driving in to see Mr Llewellyn about the new parents' advisory committee. So, Doyle got a lift right into the special car park below the Head's office. Last night he'd heard his dad talking to his mate Robo's dad about the committee. Dad was great on committees. 'What we need is a scheme in reserve . . . a Plan B to follow Plan A if it fails,' he said.

Plan A, Plan B. Doyle liked that. That was what was needed to achieve his ambition to crush P. Jenkins Esq., to atomize him, to fix him so there'd only be a dirty spot left for the old biddy with the Flash to mop up from the floor. That was what he needed, he thought, as he dressed in leisurely style . . . Plan A, Plan B, Plan C.

When they reached school, he stopped in the passage which runs alongside the staffroom. Near the ceiling was a ventilator and he knew that if he stood with his back to the wall and listened carefully, he could hear what the teachers were talking about.

You don't believe it? Well, listen.

8

Chapter 2

'Go-o-o-od morning!'

Mr Baxter, known to the troops as 'Bullet', crashed into the staffroom like a cheerful Sherman tank.

'Good morning!'

Mr Sutcliffe and Miss Peterson looked up from the papers they were working on, muttered 'Good morning' and went on with their conversation.

'Did you two sleep here last night?' asked Baxter, hurling himself into a rickety armchair which squealed under his weight.

Ignoring him, Miss Peterson asked Sutcliffe: 'What are you saying about Justin Bennett? I had his father on the phone yesterday, demanding to know how his son was getting on.'

'Demanding?'

'Yes, there was a sort of "or else" tone to it.'

Sutcliffe shook his head. 'Justin ought to be doing a lot better. Hasn't done much at all in English this term. Seems to be in a world of his own.'

'That's bad. Same in the other subjects. I get the impression Dad's thinking of taking him away from the school.'

'Oh, I thought Mrs Bennett was very involved in parent teachers . . .'

'Maybe, but Dad sounded a bit brisk. You remember he came close to taking the lad away a little while ago.'

'Pity, Justin seemed to be settling in after a rather dodgy year.'

'Ah, well,' said Miss Peterson, 'perhaps we can talk his old man round – hello, June.'

Miss Summers, the art teacher arrived, breathless.

Baxter jerked his head up.

'Ah, June. Just in time to put the kettle on.'

'Am I now?' came the answer. 'If you weren't such a male chauvinist pig, Baxter my boy, you'd see from the rota that . . .'

'The kettle's on,' interrupted Miss Peterson.

'Good-oh.' Baxter launched himself from the chair and began assembling mugs on the tea-stained table next to a small sink by the staffroom window.

The door opened and the Deputy Head looked in.

'Ah – the Head would like a few minutes with you people before . . .'

'Good lord, man,' said Baxter, 'this place gets more like a madhouse every day. Doesn't the boss know we have Year Assembly this morning – and we're supposed to teach the troops as well?'

'I know, he wants to talk to you about the assembly, and the new parents' advisory committee.'

The door closed. Everyone began to drink their tea more hastily. Baxter went on grumbling . . .

'I don't know, new form structure, new timetable, Christmas reports, school and community lark, parents' advisory committees, year assemblies . . . Democracy run riot, if you ask me.'

'Come on,' said Miss Summers, 'we've always had our year assemblies.'

'Ah that's different. In the old days *we* used to tell *them*. Now we're supposed to listen while they discuss. There'll be no end to it. Before the Welsh Wizard has finished with us, we'll have the blooming school run by parents and pupils . . .'

He looked round, cup in hand . . .

'Think of it, all of you. If that happened, what sort of TAM rating would we get, eh? Young Graham here will be OK, he'll get the female vote. But what about the likes of me?'

'But Baxter,' said Miss Summers, sweetly. 'I thought you were appreciated in the school.'

'Me, June, I'm a minority taste – BBC-2, me. But definitely not loved by the rabble. Can you imagine young Jenkins filling in my end of term report? Think what he'd say . . .'

Miss Peterson looked up seriously. 'I don't think we shall hear very much of young P.J. till term end . . .'

'What's this?' Baxter's eyes rounded. 'Has the galloping lurgy struck him down at last?'

Miss Peterson shook her head. 'The boss had him in yesterday and gave him the last warning. Any more malarkey and he's for the high jump.'

'Well that'll be the first sports event he's ever entered,' said Baxter. He slammed down his cup. 'Look at the time! Forward men – and persons too,' he smirked at Miss Summers as he flung open the staffroom door. As he stood in the corridor he bellowed:

'What are you doing there, Doyle? On your way, lad.'

But Doyle had heard all he wanted through his ventilator listening post and was already on his way down the corridor.

Any more trouble and Jenkins was for the chop, eh?

All that was needed was a little bit of trouble then wasn't it?

Chapter 3

Mr Baxter rose in his seat at the front of the Assembly Hall and leered at the rows of pupils.

'Now, if you are all settled in and relaxed, not *that* relaxed, Jenkins, this is an assembly, not an orgy, I have an announcement to make. As you know, the Head has decided to introduce a Parents' Advisory Committee with two representatives for each year.'

He tapped on the table at his side. 'Nomination papers are here. Take one before you leave. If your parents think any of their number worthy enough, or have the nerve, to sit on this committee, we must have their names by next Monday in good time for the parents' meeting before term end. Failure to fill in the form could mean your parents' ambitions for public fame will be shattered – and we don't want that, do we . . . ?'

A half hearted 'no–o–o' came from the first row. Then Doyle was on his feet.

'Sir, my father says . . .'

Baxter cut him short.

'Doyle. Everyone knows what your respected father says. How could we not? The time for election speeches is not *now*.' His voice rose: 'Just make sure your parents get these forms.'

Doyle sat down reluctantly.

'Now,' said Baxter, 'Miss Peterson has a word for your ears.'

Miss Peterson left her chair on the platform, came down

to the floor and stood close to the front row. Her face was serious.

'A word from the Head. This term has seen an unpleasant increase in guerilla warfare between Grange Hill and Brookdale School.'

Someone sniggered. Miss Peterson frowned.

'It has to stop.'

She looked briefly in Tucker's direction.

'Leading contenders on both sides have been warned. No more of that. What we want to say to *all* of you is "cool it" between now and Christmas. As far as possible, keep out of each other's way.'

'How can we do that, miss?' asked one boy. 'The Brookdale mob are always jumping our people.'

There was a murmur of agreement. Miss Peterson shook her head.

'Both schools are expected to keep away from each other. I'd suggest that since the High Road and shopping centre form a kind of natural barrier, you stay on your side, they stay on theirs – and avoid trouble, don't look for it.'

Several hands went up.

'Miss,' said Tucker, 'what about when we're doing the shopping?'

'Jenkins!' interrupted Mr Baxter. 'Let me know immediately you want to do the shopping for your mother. I'll be so intrigued I'll escort you round the Arndale myself.'

Tucker made a face but said nothing.

'Miss.'

'Yes, Penny?' said Miss Peterson.

'I have music lessons in Queen Street, the other side of Brookdale.'

'And, miss,' Cathy had her hand up – to Trisha's

astonishment. Cathy blushed, but went on : 'We may need to go across to visit – friends.'

Miss Peterson flapped her hands.

'You all know the difference between necessary trips and raiding parties. Now can we get down to our real business? Penny!'

Penny Lewis came to the platform, shuffling her notes. She was nervous, but outwardly she sounded calm.

'We thought it would be a good idea . . .' she began.

'Who did?' came a voice from the back. Baxter frowned, but Penny carried on.

'The School Council thought it would be a good idea if we had a proper friendly competition with Brookdale, instead of this stupid fighting.'

'Make love, not war,' muttered someone.

'We'd like to challenge them to a money-raising effort for charity – Spastics or Save the Children. Something worthwhile.'

There were some quiet noises of appreciation, which died away as Penny went on.

'We're suggesting a sponsored walk – up to 10p a mile according to how much parents and friends can stand. Miss Summers has agreed to register everyone and we'll provide lists for you to collect on. Mr Baxter has offered to run training sessions.'

She sat down amid chattering and mumbling.

'Sir, when will the training sessions be?' came the question.

'*After* school,' answered Baxter.

The subdued groans now grew louder. Tucker got to his feet, turning round to his mates.

'Typical of the kind of wet idea you get when women are in charge.'

14

'Jenkins, speak to the chair,' thundered Baxter.

Tucker turned to the platform.

'I said, it's typical . . .'

'We heard you, boy. If that's the only useful thing that you have to say, then sit down and shut up.'

'That's it, sir,' Tucker sounded inspired. 'That was what I was going to suggest. A sponsored silence, up to 10p a day . . .'

'You mean, Jenkins,' asked Baxter incredulously, 'that you are suggesting people don't speak at all throughout the day, not even "give over kicking my ankle", or "stop you're breaking my neck"?'

The audience roared with laughter. Tucker was furious but kept calm and even managed a touch of sarcasm.

'It's a serious proposal. I mean you keep quiet during class time, only speak when you have to, when a teacher asks you something.'

Mr Baxter was about to speak, when Miss Peterson intervened.

'I think I know what Jenkins is after. I think it's a good idea, but surely you're not suggesting this *instead* of the sponsored walk – that will still be the main effort.'

There was a noisy burst of conversation and argument, then Trisha stood up.

'Well, I for one, don't think much of either idea. They both sound a drag to me. Speaking just for myself, I'd rather eat semolina for a fortnight than go on a flipping sponsored walk.'

'That's it,' shouted someone, 'a slurp-in.'

Trisha grinned and amid the laughter spoke more loudly.

'Why not, sir? Why not have volunteers to eat semolina for school dinner? Everybody knows no one wants to. Every day, say, for a week, up to 10p a day,' she mimicked

Penny's voice.

Now the noise was deafening, cheers, boos, groans, laughs, and at the back the brilliant brigade began to make rhythmic slurping and belching sounds. Baxter slapped his hand on the table top like a pistol shot.

'Let's have a sponsored hush for ten seconds. Now, Penny, what's your verdict?'

'I honestly don't think it's going to work, with three different projects. The more we work together the more money we raise . . .

'After all, that's what the School Council worked out its proposals for, so we could work together.'

'Well, what's the assembly for, then?' interrupted Trisha.

'Hear, hear,' shouted her form mates.

Miss Peterson nodded. 'Trisha has a point. After all, this is a voluntary effort. Can I suggest now that we have three schemes, assuming they *are* all serious, that everyone thinks it over and registers with Miss Summers before the end of the week.'

'Miss.'

'Yes, Michael Doyle?'

'Miss, how about getting something in the local rag this weekend? My dad knows the Editor.'

'He would,' said Tucker, loudly. Doyle ignored him.

'It'd put Brookdale on the spot and us on the map.'

'Well,' said Baxter, 'if the Head agrees, and I'm sure he will, we'll inform the local press. A little favourable publicity for a change would do no harm. Now it is almost break time. So unless we have other business . . .'

As the assembly broke up and everyone headed for the door, pushing and arguing, Cathy nudged Trisha.

'You're a madam, you are.'

'What d'you mean?'

'You know very well what I mean. You thought that semolina rubbish up just to muck Penny Whatsit about, didn't you?'

Trisha looked faintly embarrassed.

'Well, she gets up my nose. Sponsored walk! Who does she think we are – the Girl Guides?'

She turned on Cathy.

'Anyway, what's all this about having friends over Brookdale way? The only person you've ever known over there's Madelin Tanner, and you don't want to see her, do you, after what she did to you?

'She nearly got you expelled.'

Cathy winced. 'No.'

'So what do you want to go over that way for?'

Cathy shrugged.

'I just might want to, that's all.'

'You're up to something, aren't you?'

'No-o.'

Trisha suddenly glared at Cathy. 'Suit yourself, then.' She jerked away and hurried after Miss Summers leaving Cathy standing.

Tucker spent the day recruiting members for the Sponsored Silence Team. There weren't many takers. Some thought it was a joke. Some were insulting. By the end of the afternoon, he had four names on his list, Alan, Benny, Hughes and himself. Well, it was a start, he thought. Perhaps he could bend a few arms tomorrow. There was method in his madness. A sponsored silence, if he had a few mates in it with him, could be just the way to keep out of bother till term end. And that he needed.

As Alan, Benny and he were leaving school, they stopped by the zebra crossing. Alan nudged Tucker and pointed across the road.

'There he is again.'

17

'Who?'

'The flasher in the car.'

Tucker looked sideways at the parked car and its rain-coated driver.

'That's not a flasher,' he said. 'That's the Old Bill.'

'The police? Get off,' said Benny. 'In that old car?'

'I'm telling you,' said Tucker.

Well, was he right? Let's see.

Chapter 4

In the local police station, not half a mile from where Tucker and his mates were walking, sat PC Benson, fat and grey-haired. Feet up on a stool, his helmet on the desk at his side, he drank tea noisily and enjoyably. The inner door swung open. Sergeant Harris, grey-haired like Benson, but leaner and smarter, came in. As a sign of respect, Benson lifted one leg down from the stool.

'One in the pot for you, Sarge.'

Harris grinned. 'I will say this for you, Alf. There is no one in the force that can make a better cup of tea than you.'

Benson nodded. 'In all my years I have learned two things of importance . . .'

Harris interrupted.

'. . . make a good cup of tea and keep the leg muscles relaxed.'

He glanced sideways at Benson's legs.

'The old feet are in good odour today.'

Benson put down his leg and reached for his helmet.

'I'll be off. Someone has to represent the visible face of the law round here. Of course, I'm only your old steam-powered copper, but . . .'

The sergeant craned his neck to look out of the window.

'As you say, Alf, but lo and behold, here comes your original solar-powered policeman.'

'What, him?' Benson looked disagreeably at the door.

'Det-con. Houston, no less,' replied the sergeant, 'known

in his own manor as Oozlem, because of his habit of flying round and round in ever-decreasing circles . . .'

Benson stood up. 'If only he would vanish . . .'

Harris grinned: 'Come on, Alf, bear it like a man. Another month till your old oppo Charlie comes off the sick and Houston flies back to his own patch.'

'A month?'

The sergeant nodded. 'No less. You, old lad, are worried in case he puts the uniformed branch to shame by clearing every case on the books before he leaves.'

Benson made a face. 'You know, Sarge, in all my time I could count the number of collars I've made on the fingers of one hand.'

'True, Alf, but you've given some awful warnings in your time and some of the people who received 'em were never the same again.'

Benson smiled fatly and Harris straightened up as a tall, thin man in a raincoat and trilby came into the room.

'Mr Houston, good afternoon.'

Det-con. Houston said nothing in reply but headed for the tea-pot. muttering to himself as a thin stream of black fluid half filled his cup.

'Was that you I saw by the zebra near Grange Hill School just now?' asked Benson, with one eye on the sergeant. 'Standing in for the lollipop lady?'

'If you must know,' Houston answered reluctantly, 'I was watching one or two characters.'

'Oh they're all characters around here, that's why we like the manor.'

'I'm talking about the school. There are one or two that bear a little detailed observation.'

Sergeant Harris leaned on the desk. 'Like who, Mr Houston?'

Houston looked at him suspiciously, then said:

'There's a little dusky boy, well, light brown. Looks as though it might be a mixed marriage.'

'Oh,' said Benson, 'you mean his mother comes from Scotland?'

Houston stared him down. 'You know what I mean. He's up to something. I saw him messing around the shops at 7 o'clock this morning.'

'Oh him,' said Benson. 'That's young Green. His dad's on the Social . . .'

'Oh yes? Is he now?'

'Yes. Hurt his back on the docks. Can't work. I expect the lad's doing the newspapers.'

'Thought he might be,' answered Houston, 'and he's under age, can't be 13 yet.'

The sergeant shrugged. 'Well that's not our problem. That's the social worker's.'

'Well, I'm keeping an eye on him. Those jobs we haven't put on anybody yet . . .'

'Which jobs?'

'Those "no visible trace of entry" jobs. I was looking at the files. Every one of the houses that got done had kids who go to Grange Hill.'

'Surprise. Most of 'em do round here.'

Houston tapped his fingers on the table.

'I reckon whoever's doing those jobs is being let into the house by someone.'

Harris frowned. 'You may be right. I still think it's someone coming in from the next manor. Someone with a bit of form but not much. Someone we don't know properly yet.'

Houston smiled thinly.

'There's one who might fit – friend of the coloured boy

21

– budding tearaway. His brother's just got a job on the building site in Broadwood Road. And the older one's got form.'

'Oh, him,' said Benson, 'Jenkins, you mean. All the form his brother's got is one drunk and disorderly and a malicious damage.'

'Ah,' said the sergeant, 'no more than anyone with red blood in his veins. But, carry on, Mr Houston, who else do we have on file?'

Houston looked for a moment as if he'd not answer, then:

'There's a funny 'un. Posh little kid, pale face, long black hair. Name of Bennett.'

'Them,' said Benson, 'they come from up the hill. Very respectable family.'

'Oh, yes?' said Houston. 'Well, what's he want down Kettlewell Street, poking in people's letter boxes?'

There was no answer.

Houston triumphantly drained his cup of tea and choked on a mouthful of tea leaves.

Chapter 5

While the police force were discussing him, Justin Bennett was in Kettlewell Street again, by the front door of the old three-storey house. He reached through the letter box, just an oblong hole in the front door, and pulled out the key on its string. As he opened the door he stood a moment in the passage. The paper was stained and peeling from the walls and the whole house smelt of damp and old cabbage water. How could people bear to live here? he wondered. He swallowed, then called.

'Mrs Carter.'

There was no answer.

'Mrs Carter,' he called more loudly.

'Is that you, Justin, love?' The weak old voice came from inside the house. 'Come in, I've got a cup of tea ready.'

Justin tip-toed down the passage. He didn't know why, but he always did. At the foot of some stairs he pushed open the door. Inside the kitchen, on a chair wedged between table and sink, sat an old woman. Her hair was snow white, her skin smooth, her eyes bright and blue. She was enormously fat. As Justin entered she turned in her seat, bracing one hand on the table and the other on the sink. She gave him a big smile then put her hand to her mouth.

'Sorry, love, forgotten my teeth.'

Justin sat down. She poured the tea. He didn't really like it. Mrs Carter made it three times as strong as his mother did. But he drank it all the same.

'Had a good day?'

'Not bad, thank you.' He fiddled with the straps of his bag.

'Got something more for me, eh?' said the old lady.

He turned red and smiled.

'Come on, let's see.'

He pulled from his bag a big scrap book, the corners strengthened with coloured plastic. On the front was written: 'Grange Hill 1909-1979 – Memories'. He opened it and carefully turned the pages, filled with his own hand-writing, with old brown photographs, newspaper cuttings, coloured postcards. She stopped him.

'Have you got any room left at the beginning?'

'A bit, maybe.'

'There's something I just remembered. I always say that. But when you're 78, you can't remember what you had for breakfast but you can remember everything that happened when you were young. It was during the War, the Great War, you know, 1914-18. We were working on munitions, for the Front. There was a powder they put in the shells, it turned your face yellow. I remember the fellers didn't want to go out with the shell-girls. That's how I met my Harold. He said the first time we went out "Oh, I don't mind, I expect you're lovely underneath" – cheeky article! Do you think I should put that in? I mean if other people are going to see it. Do I embarrass you, love?'

Justin shook his head and blushed again.

'Well, you please yourself, love. You're writing it.'

'It is your story, though.'

'Ah, but you're putting it down. You are clever. Your mum and dad must be proud of you. Would you like an-other cup, Justin?'

'No thanks, Mrs Carter.'

'Well, shall we have our walk then? Here's the key.'
Justin leapt up from the table, stowed away the scrapbook and hurried out to the front door. Behind him, Mrs Carter slowly struggled to her feet.

He was not allowed to help her.

Outside he jumped down the steps and taking the key Mrs Carter had given him he opened a little side door and dragged out a battered old wheelchair. By the time he had it on the pavement, Mrs Carter was heaving herself slowly down the steps, clinging to the iron rail that ran by the side.

'Where shall we go? To the park?'

'All right.'

Justin hauled at the chair, while Mrs Carter pushed on the large wheel rims at the sides. Soon they were moving down the road. But it was a slow walk. The chair was heavy and they had to stop every few yards for Mrs Carter to greet friends and neighbours. In the park at last, she twisted her head round to look at him.

'They wanted me to pack up and leave the area when Harold died after the War – the second one I mean. But I wouldn't go. I'll die and be buried here, or go up in a puff of smoke at the crematorium. Do you know, the other day, some lads, real ruffians, threw stones at my wall. I went out – I did you know – and shouted at them. Next door said: "I don't know how you dare do it," but I did. They won't get me out of here unless I want to go.'

Justin nodded. The walk was extra long that day and he was later home than usual. His mother met him in the hall. He remembered the nomination papers.

'Are you going to stand for the parents' committee, Mum?'

She looked bothered.

'Yes, Justin, I think so. I hope so. Justin, we'd – your father wants to have a word with you about possibly changing schools next term. I'm afraid he's not very pleased with the way you're getting on, at Grange Hill.'

Chapter 6

Cathy didn't wait for Trisha, that afternoon. She ran through the cloaks, snatched up her coat and was away from school while the others were yakking away. She had two good reasons why she didn't want to walk home with Trisha. For one, Trish couldn't talk about anything but this flipping semolina slurp-in. She was going round all day getting it fixed up – and Miss Peterson seemed to be encouraging her. She'd even been talking to the cook in the canteen. Had they got enough of the muck in stock? How stupid could you get? And all because she had this nark on over Penny Templeton Lewis. Penny did get up your nose a bit. She was cool. She always knew things. And she was so nice it made you feel peculiar sometimes. But so what? She was like that. Trish was no soap advert herself for that matter.

Besides, the second reason was more important. The second reason was Neil. He was at Brookdale. He must be months younger than her. In English with Mr Sutcliffe, they'd just started *Romeo and Juliet*. It just fitted. Neil and her, and the Brookdale and Grange Hill kids fighting it out. And her having to keep it secret. They'd better not touch Neil, he wasn't really big enough to look after himself. He was smaller than her as well as younger. Suddenly she forgot about *Romeo and Juliet* and imagined she was the Bionic Woman, jumping from a blazing building, holding Neil under one arm. She whizzed through the air, all bionic limbs going.

'Look out, you – !'

27

She opened her eyes. She was balanced on the edge of the pavement opposite the shopping centre. She'd nearly stepped under a truck.

'Sorry.'

She walked to the crossing and over into the centre.

Outside the sky was beginning to darken, but here all the windows blazed with lights and Christmas decorations. She strolled from shop to shop, wondering if she could find a present for Neil, until she reached the sheltered arcade where they'd – well, half said they'd meet.

But there was no Neil. She hung about for a few minutes. It hadn't been a hard and fast arrangement, but she'd been so sure. After a while she moved on to the Brookdale side of the centre. It was darker still outside now after the light from the shops. She'd have to go home soon. Perhaps she'd walk down the road towards the school a bit. He might have been kept in. There was no one around to see who she was. And anyway with no school uniforms these days you had to look closely to see who was who.

She had gone a couple of hundred yards down the road when she heard her name called. She turned. Someone was running after her, breathlessly.

'Cathy!'

It was Neil!

She turned back and they almost bumped into one another.

'Cathy, I'm sorry. Didn't mean to be late.'

'That's no excuse.' She pretended to be severe, then was sorry at the look on his face. She put her arm through his and they walked on.

'Cathy, I can't stay. Our little kid's sick. I've been out to phone the doctor. I have to go back now. Mum won't be home till five o'clock.'

She was disappointed, but said:

'That's all right, Neil.'

'Shall we see – tomorrow?' he asked shyly. 'Tell you what, how about lunch-time? Shall I come over your way?'

'No, I'll come here.' She mustn't let the Grange Hill mob get their paws on Neil. *Romeo and Juliet* again. 'Where shall we meet?'

'There's a kids' recreation ground just across the road here. We can sit in the shelter. See you,' he called as he ran.

She made a kiss with her lips as he vanished and then turned in the darkened street and hurried back to the bright lights.

But as she reached a cross street, two figures moved across to block her way. They were lads, taller than her, fifteen or sixteen at least. She felt a sudden cold in her stomach and moved off the pavement to go round them. But they blocked her way again.

'Just a minute, Cathy,' said one.

She stared.

'I don't know you, do I?'

'No, but we know you, and we don't like you.'

'I don't know what you're talking about.' Cathy tried to be calm, looking round to see if she could run somewhere.

'We don't like coppers' narks,' went on the lad. 'Nobody likes coppers' narks.'

There was someone coming up behind them.

Cathy turned.

'Excuse me,' she said.

'What's up, Cathy, darling? Did the nasty boys frighten you?'

Standing a yard away from her was Madelin Tanner.

Chapter 7

Madelin took Cathy's arm. In the dying light her face looked pale, sharp and mean. Her grip on the arm was painful as she steered Cathy towards the shopping centre. The lads walked on either side of her.

'That's OK, fellers. Cathy and I are going to have a little talk, just girls together.'

'Oh yes? Suppose she does a bunk or screams for the law?' asked one.

Madelin laughed. 'Not her. She's wetting her pants now in case someone sees me with her in the shops.' She glanced sideways at Cathy. 'S'all right, dear. We're not going on the rob today, like we used to, just having a little chat while we walk round. So, do us a favour, fellers, just vanish a bit. She'll be very good.'

As they reached the shops, Madelin's grip on Cathy's arm tightened, but she chatted casually, as though they were school friends shopping. From the corner of her eye, Cathy saw that Madelin was dressed in a white trouser suit with a bright red and yellow scarf at her thoat. It was smart in a way, but grubby. Her hair had been tinted and it made her face look older. The narrow lips were tight and red. There was something miserable about her, but frightening at the same time.

'They'll not touch you, while I'm around. They do what I tell them, mostly. They don't come from round here, see, and they need me to show them where things are, don't they? The big one's a frightener, isn't he, but he's not bad really. It's the thin one you want to watch. He puts the dreads up me, sometimes.'

'I don't know what you're telling me this for,' said Cathy, looking round.

'No use looking for someone you know, love. If they see you with naughty Madelin, who got taken away because she went on the rob they'll say to themselves "tut tut, that bad Cathy Hargreaves, she made out she was led on by that Tanner girl, when all the time" . . .'

She halted Cathy by a jeweller's window.

'Has he offered to buy you a ring?'

'Who?'

'Your lovely little boy friend. Oh we've had our eye on you, Cathy. You're a little raver on the quiet, aren't you, sneaking off like this with a boy from Brookdale. What would Auntie Trisha say to that?'

'If she saw you, she'd probably poke you one,' said Cathy.

Madelin sniggered and pinched Cathy.

'She might, too. I don't like things like that, though. That's why I have my friends with me.'

'What have you been doing lately, Madelin?' Cathy tried to keep her voice level.

'Aren't you crafty? Changing the subject. Look, let's not talk about it. Let's say that these past few months I've had a lot of attention from some very nice people, a lot more than Grange Hill or my mum ever gave me, and I've learnt a lot. What do they call it? I've graduated. I've passed out, that's it. They used to think I was a failure, a slow learner. But I'm not you know. I caught on very fast. I'm a bright girl. Just a late developer. And you know what, Cathy? They think I'm just about ready to come back to Grange Hill. You'd like that, wouldn't you?'

'What do you want, Madelin?' Nervousness made Cathy's voice sharp.

31

'What do I want? Nothing. Well nothing at the moment.'

Madelin smirked at Cathy. 'I don't even bear you a grudge for dropping me in it over that lucky dip we had in the boutique that time. I don't even feel bitter at you for shopping me, for making out it was me who started it all.'

'It was.'

'That's your story. Anyway, don't let's fall out. Let's be friends. We'll be seeing each other a lot now.'

'We won't, you know.'

'We will, you know.'

They were standing by the zebra on the Grange Hill side of the centre, now. Madelin gave Cathy a last painful nip and pushed her into the road. A car braked to let her stagger over the crossing.

At the wheel of the car, Mrs Templeton Lewis, who had just picked up her daughter from her music lesson, said to Penny:

'Careless child, I could have knocked her down. Is she from your school, Penny?'

'Yes. It's Cathy Hargreaves, Trisha's friend, you know.'

'Ah!' Penny's mother let in the clutch.

'And who was that rather over-dressed girl talking to her?'

'I'm not sure,' answered Penny.

But she was. She had recognized Madelin.

Tucker fans, both of you, don't be impatient. Just read on. Next page – dimbo!

Chapter 8

A minute after they had spotted Det-con. Houston at the zebra near school, Tucker Jenkins and his mates had forgotten all about him. As they strolled, pushed and shoved their way along the crowded pavements, Benny was talking about his dad's invalid car, due to be delivered that day.

'That should be a help,' said Alan.

'Help, you're joking, this is the best thing in years, man,' answered Benny.

'What is?' asked Tucker, whose mind was elsewhere.

'Dad's car.'

'Hey, your dad got wheels, eh? You'll be able to get around now.'

'Pin-brain,' said Benny. 'It only holds one.'

'One? What good's that? Might as well have a bike.'

'Lots of good to my dad. Now maybe he can get a job.'

'Hey, great!' Tucker punched Benny on the shoulder. 'What'll he do?'

Benny shrugged. 'Depends. Lots he can't do. Not many places will look at him.'

'Yeah,' said Alan. 'Any case, there aren't many jobs going for anybody. Lots of kids can't even get jobs when they leave school.'

'Get off,' jeered Tucker, 'you worried about that already? Hey, our kid's got a job on that building site in Broadwood. Drives a dumper and things. Ace. D'you reckon that'd be something for your dad, Benbo? He was a crane driver, wasn't he?'

'Was,' said Benny. 'He couldn't get up the ladders now. Don't reckon he'd do it even if they let him. No, he'll be looking for something like lift-man, gate-keeper, you know, where you can sit down a bit. Hey look.'

He pointed at the window of a car accessory shop. 'That's what I'm getting our dad for Christmas. Tool kit.'

They crowded to the window. Tucker stared. 'That's ten quid. Where'd you get that kind of money, Benbo?'

'I give 'em £1.50 then 50p a week till it's paid off.'

'Where'd you get your £1.50?' Tucker was curious.

'I'll have it by the weekend.'

'Oh, yeah?'

'Yeah,' Benny looked away. 'I'm helping this bloke with his newspaper round. I mean we split it and he gives me half. I get 75p a week. Well, it's better than nothing. I mean they won't let me have a round myself – I tried it before and they said I was too young.'

'So that's where you go mornings, eh? Who's the bloke?'

Benny looked away again.

'A bloke.'

Tucker was suspicious. But all he said was: 'Be like that. Hey, are you two coming round to Broadwood? I'm going to see our kid.'

Both shook their heads. Alan added, 'I'm going to have a look at Benny's dad's car, then home.'

'You two are useless – what are you?'

Tucker wandered off leaving his mates still peering into the shop window and slipped across the road into a side street, leading to Broadwood Road. This lay behind the flats where his family lived. From his bedroom, Tucker could look down on the building site. It was fantastic. A great hole in the ground, littered with gear, two huge cranes across the skyline, bulldozers and dumpers cruising up and down like space buggies on Mars, blokes swinging on girders, shouting, buzzers going. And often in the dark evenings, huge floodlights would light the whole area up. His mum and dad couldn't wait to see the back of the whole business. But for Tucker it was great. He could watch it for hours. Now his brother was working there, he might get to go inside.

He stood at the site gates. The place was ablaze with light. It made the evening sky even darker. Then he saw the truck, just inside the gates, parked near the high mesh fence. It was massive and red, with a high seat and great wheels and gears. No one was around. He sidled through the gate opening and nipped quickly over to the dumper. One foot on the wheel hub and he was in the driving seat. Or nearly.

Just as he was balanced, one leg in the air, a cheerful Irish voice boomed out behind him :

'And what do you think you're at?'

Chapter 9

Tucker lost balance and fell. His head donged on the truck wheel and he landed, dizzy, on his back. A hand as big as a shovel picked him up and another dusted him down. It was like being groomed with an excavator bucket. He looked up – it hurt his neck – and saw a massive grey-haired chest half covered by a check shirt, then a red face and a bald head. The big voice spoke again.

'What are you doing here, lad? Don't you know kids can get killed on building sites?'

'Looking for my brother, sir.'

'And who's he?'

'His name's Jenkins.'

'Ah, and you're Tucker?'

Tucker gawped.

'Yes – sir.'

'You don't have to call me sir, just call me Paddy.'

'Don't let him put you on, our kid,' said a voice nearby. 'He's got the most clout on this job.'

Both looked round. Tucker's brother sat in the truck seat.

'Paddy's the shop steward, Tucker. It's a toss up who's more scared of him – the guv'nor or us.'

Paddy smiled. 'Your brother and the truth are old friends, Tucker – they meet just now and then.'

Tucker stared at the two of them. He'd always thought his brother was tough, but this bloke would have made two of him and then some.

'Listen, Jenks, they want the dumper over the other side.

But some person has mislaid the keys.'

Tucker's brother flapped a hand. 'Not to worry. What're the distributor leads for?'

Paddy shook his huge head. 'There's education for you. Don't you know there's a right way and a wrong way of doing things?'

'Your trouble is, Paddy, you're so straight they use you for a spirit level.'

'And you're a little too smart for your own good.' Paddy beckoned and Tucker's brother climbed from the seat, jumping down beside them.

'Someone has been keeping an eye on you, Jenks.'

'Who?' Tucker saw his brother's grin vanish.

'The law.'

'Ah, not to worry. Old Benson's so slow he thinks copper nitrate is his overtime payments.'

'It's not PC Benson, Jenks, but a gent in a raincoat in an old car parked just down the way. Name of Houston.'

'How d'you know, Paddy?'

'Because I'm a sociable chap and I have a pint with Benson now and then. Incidentally,' he looked down at Tucker, 'I also have a chat now and then with an old acquaintance of yours. He's told me a thing or two.'

'Who's that?' Now Tucker was suspicious.

'Why Mr Garfield, the respected caretaker at Grange Hill.'

'Oh him. Don't believe a word he says. He's all bitter and twisted.'

'On the contrary, a decent, amiable man.'

'You've got the wrong bloke, Paddy.'

'Does it ever occur to you, Tucker, that working all day with hundreds of characters like yourself might sour a man somewhat?'

Tucker grinned and said nothing. His brother sprang up in the saddle again.

'Thanks for the tip, Paddy. But they've got nothing on me.'

He bent down under the steering wheel.

'What about those keys, Jenks?' Paddy roared, but his voice was drowned as the engine came to life and Tucker's brother swung the dumper away with a grinding of gears.

Paddy shook his head.

'Now and again your brother is a little too fast for his own health.' He looked down at Tucker.

'What do you plan to do with yourself when you leave school?'

Tucker looked round.

'Wouldn't mind working on the building. I like woodwork, painting, things like that.'

'You could do better, Tucker, with education.'

'What's wrong with the building, Paddy? You do it.'

'Nothing, but if you want to go anywhere, these days, education is the thing. You make the most of it, lad.'

With a pat on the shoulder which also pushed Tucker half through the gates, Paddy walked away, whistling. Tucker ran home.

That night in bed, he dreamt he was driving the dumper, carrying Doyly bound hand and foot towards a deep hole in the ground. He woke up in darkness. The luminous dial on the battered old clock by his bed showed 6.30. For a second he tried to sleep again, then changed his mind.

He'd remembered about Benny.

Chapter 10

Tucker dressed in the dark and crept downstairs. No one else was awake yet. Outside it was so cold he almost changed his mind and went back to bed. But curiosity was stronger. At seven he was hiding in a side passage opposite Benny's house. It was still dark but the street lamp gave some light. Suddenly he felt embarrassed spying on his mate. But he couldn't go back now. He waited.

After five minutes, there was Benny, slipping out of the house, zipping up his jacket, blowing on his hands. He moved quickly, and Tucker had to shift to keep him in sight. When Benny slowed down, he dodged inside a garden gate, then dodged out again when some early riser thumped on the window.

Benny turned right at the shops. Tucker accelerated. Then screeched to a halt. Across the road, parked opposite the T-junction was the old car – the law, the bloke he and his mates called Flash Harry. What was he up to – tailing Benny, tailing their kid? Then he thought – what am I doing? I'm doing the same as him.

Tucker peered round the corner, then jerked back. Benny was talking to an older kid outside the newsagent's. Had Benny seen him? He leaned forward again. No, Benny was still talking. Correction, they were arguing. Then the bigger kid picked up a large bag and humped it on to his shoulder and they went off together.

So that was what Benbo was up to, helping with a newspaper round. And that was why he was saying nothing. The bloke he was helping was Macker's elder brother.

And Macker was Doyle's sidekick. No wonder Benny kept quiet. And pound to a peanut he was being ripped off.

On impulse, Tucker nipped into the shop. A grey-haired man was sorting magazines at the counter. He looked up over his glasses.

'Yes?'

'Want any newspapers delivered, mister?'

'How old are you?'

'Twelve.' Tucker spoke without thinking.

'Come back next year, son.'

Tucker screwed up his face.

'Ah, I wanted to make a bit before Christmas, mister.'

'Sorry, son, you're too young.'

'How much d'you pay?'

'£2.50 a week – that's Saturdays and Sundays as well.'

'OK. Thanks. I'll come back.'

Tucker walked home slowly. He was no mathematical genius. At £2.50 a week it was a rip off. But if Benny was sharing that round for 75p a week, it was a carve up.

As he made his way to school later, he passed the building site in Broadwood Road. He thought of Paddy and wondered what the big man would do with a problem like Benny's. First of all, though, he'd have a word with Benbo.

Charging down the corridor in school, his eye caught the notice board. The notices were up for the sponsored events. He stopped and checked. Fifty for the Walk, 20 for the Slurp-in and 4 for the Silence. He blew a raspberry at the board and barged on into the classroom. Benny was late and Tucker couldn't get him on his own until break. Then he tackled him about the newspapers. At first Benny didn't want to talk. He was angry at being followed. Then he admitted he was being ripped off.

'Tucker, I need the money.'

'Yeah, but 75p isn't right, is it, Benbo? You do half the work, he gets most of the bread.'

Benny was embarrassed.

'What can I do, Tucker?'

Tucker thought quickly. What would Paddy do?

'Tell him he can stuff his round.'

'He'll get somebody else.'

'Tell him first thing tomorrow. He won't have time, will he?'

Benny looked doubtful.

'Look, kid, I'll come with you. I'll do the shop steward thing on him.'

'Will you?'

Tucker slapped Benny on the shoulder.

Getting up at 6.30 again next morning was rough. But the old alarm worked. He was awake like a shot, killed it at one blow, staggered into his clothes and down the stairs. By seven he was outside the newsagent's with Benny, waiting for Macker's brother. Tucker braced himself for a row and thought of Paddy. But things didn't quite go as he expected.

At first Macker's brother was shaken. Then he acted tough. For a second Tucker was scared, but he stood his ground. The argument got fierce. The newsagent came to his door and called out. Macker's brother picked up his bag and made to move off.

'You coming, Greenie?'

Tucker grabbed Benny's arm and held him fast.

'Your last chance, Snowball.'

Macker's brother paused a second. Then he gave them two fingers and vanished round the corner.

Benny pulled loose from Tucker's grip.

'You're a big help,' he said.

Chapter 11

That afternoon, as Tucker wandered along Broadwood Road he heard his name called. Big Paddy was standing at the site gate.

'Now then, Tucker. How's it going?'

Tucker shrugged.

'Where's your mate, Benny?'

Tucker made a face. Paddy beckoned him. 'What's up, lad?'

Tucker hesitated, then told the story of the newspapers. Paddy laughed, till the ground shook. Then he was serious.

'You are just like your brother and the other young blokes on this firm. Always having a go before they've weighed up the odds. See, Tucker. The feller who does the round – he's the employer. Your mate Benny's the workforce. That is unless Benny and the other feller ask the newsagent for a rise?'

'Huh,' said Tucker. 'Can't see that happening.'

'Right. So who needs who the most?'

'Benbo needs the money. His dad's on the Social.'

Paddy nodded. 'Ah, Mr Green's the one with the back, isn't he?'

Tucker thought again.

'But Macker's brother must need Benny or he wouldn't have asked him in the first place.'

'Right, but don't forget, Tucker. This other feller has the round. Benny's under age. He shouldn't really be doing it. Personally I'm against kids working. It'd be a lot

42

better if Benny's old man had a job.'

'Ah, that's all right for you to talk, Paddy.'

'Right, Tucker. It's easy for me to say. But unless you can find some other card to play, Benny either gives in or he sweats it out till the other feller does.'

Tucker walked home slowly, chewing it over.

Next morning he was on the streets again in the half dark. Only this time he was following Macker's brother, not Benny. He kept a careful distance behind him, for half an hour, then ran back home. Next morning at first light, he was out again, slipping from door to door, making sure no one saw him.

Later that day as he came in for registration, Benny met him, his face split in a big grin.

'Hey, Tucker. What d'you know. Macker's brother came round our place.'

'He did?' Tucker sounded surprised.

'He's been having a hard time. He can't get the round done in time. And he's been messing things up, mixing the papers.'

'Get away!'

'Hey, and he asked me if I'd do it again – for a quid.'

Tucker said:

'You didn't agree, did you?'

Benny stared. 'Why not? Look, Tucker, I need the money.'

'Benbo. Don't be stupid. Stick it out. He's bound to give in.'

'You can talk, Tucker. It's not up to you, is it, man?'

'See, Benny. Give him another day. Let him sweat.'

Benny agreed. But Tucker could see he didn't like it.

Next morning Tucker was finishing his little operation, slipping the *Sun* from one letter box, the *Telegraph* from another and switching them, when he felt a hand on his collar. He leapt a foot in the air. Behind him was the man in the raincoat.

'What are you up to, my lad?'

He thought quickly. 'They brought us the wrong paper, mister. I was just putting it right.'

The man stared. Then nodded.

'All right. But watch it.'

On his way home from school he spotted Paddy again near the site fence. He shouted and the big man came over. He grinned when Tucker told him what had happened.

'So, you're holding out for the jackpot, are you, Tucker? Well, take a bit of advice. Don't forget it's Benny who's at the sharp end, not you. He has the last word.'

He paused.

'Anyway, Tucker. Tell Benny there might be a job for his dad. Light work. The firm needs a bloke, pensioner or someone to go round every afternoon, check the sheds and gates on all the sites. He could do it. It's not security stuff, they've an agency for that. So, just let him know, eh?'

Tucker thanked Paddy and hurried off. At Benny's house no one answered. He ripped a page out of an exercise book and wrote a note about the job, pushed it through the door and went home.

Next morning he stayed in bed. He overslept and got to school just in time for registration.

'Hey, Benbo,' he called. 'Get my note?'

Benny didn't seem to hear. He turned his back on Tucker.

'Hey, what's with you?' Tucker asked.

Benny rounded on him.

'Macker's brother got the push, that's what. He'd been warned. It wasn't his fault. Some joker messed the papers up again today.'

'Serve him right, anyway,' said Tucker.

'You crazy?' yelled Benny. 'What about me? I get the push as well, don't I?'

'Heck,' said Tucker.

Chapter 12

The weekend was a dead loss. There wasn't even enough homework to make the time pass. Benny wouldn't come out – he nearly shut the door in Tucker's face. Tucker sloped down to the site on Broadwood but couldn't spot Paddy or his brother. Roaming round the edge of the building site, he found a spot where the mesh fence had come adrift from the posts. You could squeeze through there. He noted that but didn't go near the fence. These days he had the feeling of being watched all the time.

Sunday dragged by, Monday came and he trundled off to school. The only good thing was only ten more suffering days to Christmas and so far he'd kept out of trouble at school. He didn't know why he bothered, though. Was Grange Hill so marvellous he should worry if they gave him the toe end? There were his mates of course – those he had left. But apart from anything his dad would murder him if Llewellyn called him in again. So, he had to stick it out.

As he got to school the place was in an uproar, with a crowd pushing and shoving round the notice board. Tucker fought his way through to the wall. It was incredible. Above the sponsored events list someone had written in pen: Slurp-in 80; Sponsored Walk 40; Silence 3. Silence three? Benny must have dropped out. Big deal. He wouldn't be talking to Tucker anyway. Then Tucker's eye caught the cutting from the local paper – front-page headlines marked out with big red ink crosses.

'Semolina Sensation! – Grange Hill Pupils'
Slurp-in for Charity.'

There was a mug-shot of Pongo Yates, grinning like
an idiot. 'Well known for her campaigning for pupil rights
in the school.'

At the bottom of the story there were two paragraphs
about the Sponsored Walk; and about the Silence – not a
thing.

Outraged, Tucker fought his way clear of the crowd
and stormed into the classroom. Doyle and his mob were
there, grinning like chimpanzees.

Tucker opened his mouth to say something when Doyle
turned, smiled sweetly at him and put a finger to his lips.
At that instant in walked Miss Peterson.

'Hello, Peter. Breaking the silence already?'

Tucker felt a head of steam build up inside him. Doyle
spoke.

'Oh, no miss. He didn't say anything. He wanted to,
but he didn't.' Macker and Robo, the creeps, sniggered.

Miss Peterson called for order and began taking the
register. Then she called Trisha Yates to the front. Grinning,
she announced:

'So many have joined the slurp-in I have to explain the
rules again. You sign on for a week. No less. You're allowed a spoonful of white or brown sugar from the counter, on each plateful. You show the empty plate to the
dinner lady afterwards.'

Someone raised their hand.

'Where's the school getting all this semolina from?'

Trisha answered. 'A supplier is donating the extra
semolina. They've promised to double anything we raise
for charity. Councillor Doyle fixed it up.'

Miss Peterson beckoned to Tucker.

'Do you want to say anything about your sponsored event, Peter?'

Reluctantly, Tucker announced: 'You can ask teachers questions. You can answer questions. But any other talking in class disqualifies you. You get a signature on your book from each subject teacher and one from Miss Peterson at the end of the day.'

He went back to his desk. Doyly was smiling and whispering. He couldn't tell what was being said, but he could guess.

Benny wouldn't even look his way, but on his desk was a note. It said: 'With you all the way man.' He turned round and Hughes gave him the thumbs-up sign.

The first period went by slowly but without any bother. He could hear Doyle's mob talking behind him, but he didn't turn round. They were out to get him and he wouldn't give an inch. He stuck his head in his book. For once it seemed interesting.

Next period was in the biology lab. Miss Dawson was grey-haired and somewhat deaf. Tucker knew there'd be trouble. And there was. Doyle and Macker began to talk about him. They weren't whispering any more. When Miss Dawson came near they stopped, then started again. Suddenly he'd had enough. He got out a sheet of graph paper, scribbled on it, stuck his ruler through the sheet and held it up. For a second there was dead silence, then Miss Dawson said quietly:

'Peter Jenkins, kindly put your – poster away.' She looked over her glasses. 'Apart from anything else, the first word is spelt wrongly, though "off" and "Doyle" are correct.'

The class laughed and then there was silence. Miss Dawson came past and bent over his desk. In her neat script she wrote in Tucker's rough work book.

'Don't be provoked, Peter!'

But worse was to come.

In history, Doyle put his hand up.

'Sir, can I ask a question?'

Mr Streatfield eyed him coldly.

'Is it about the Middle Ages, Doyle?'

'No, sir, more about the 18th century.'

'Is it really important?'

'I just wanted to ask about that war with Spain. I mean the one they started because a bloke said he'd had his ear cut off.'

'Ah, you mean the War of Jenkins' Ear, Doyle?'

Laughter began all round Tucker. He gritted his teeth.

Doyle went on. 'It seems a bit stupid to me, sir. And I read somewhere that this bloke Jenkins was a liar anyway.'

Tucker felt the steam rising from the top of his head. But he stuck his head back in his book and waited for the laughter to die down. By lunch-time he was ready to explode. What made it worse was that Benny and Alan had both joined the slurp-in. The semolina table was crowded. Everyone was joking and shouting to one another.

Out on the field Bullet Baxter was running a training session for Penny and about a dozen other girls. He looked sick. Tucker knew how he felt. After lunch, the needling in class began again. Tucker knew he'd have to do something about it before the day was out. But what?

The last two periods were English. Mr Sutcliffe came in, bright-eyed and bushy-tailed as usual, full of the Christmas Literary Competition.

'Anyone who hasn't begun to work, but still wants to take part, can use this double period. Stories, essays, poems on the theme of "Grange Hill". Only let me know what you're planning to do.'

Tucker put his hand up.

'Could I enter a poem about Grange Hill, sir?'

Sutcliffe's eyes opened wide.

'About the school?'

'Yes, sir.'

'Something I can let the Head see?'

'Of course, sir.'

'Carry on then.'

There was silence for a second, then Robo said:

'This should be good.'

And Doyle added: 'I can hardly wait to see it.'

'All right. Let's have some hush, back there,' warned Sutcliffe.

The class settled down. The silence deepened as people got on with their work. Time passed. Tucker chewed his pen and looked at the ceiling. Behind he heard Doyle whisper.

' "S-k-o-o-l" spells school, Jenkins.'

Tucker turned and slowly raised two fingers, then turned back and began to write. Five minutes before the end of the afternoon, he suddenly raised his hand.

'Sir, have we got time for me to read my poem?'

'Surely it can't be finished, Peter?'

'Well, just one verse, sir. A sample. I'd like to get the opinion of the class before I go any further.'

Sutcliffe looked wary.

'Very well, Peter.'

Tucker rose, looked round at the silent class and began to read, slowly and with dignity, stressing the end word of each line.

'In Grange Hill School we pupils toil,
Until our brains we need to oil,
Before our heads begin to boil,

50

There's only one thing that can spoil,
A fat, disgusting little boil,
His name is Michael, Big-Head . . .'

As the class round him yelled out 'Doyle!' Tucker walked up to Mr Sutcliffe.

'Could you kindly sign my silence book, sir?' he asked loudly.

Chapter 13

The staffroom door crashed open and Baxter rolled in.

'June!' he bellowed.

Miss Summers looked up from her chair.

'Was there something . . .?'

'Yes there was. You have to do something about these sponsored events. There are only 20 left on the walk.'

'Baxter, dear, I've told them we are not signing any more on for semolina after today. But more I cannot do. You cannot make anyone sign for anything and you know it.'

'Well, it's absurd,' muttered Baxter.

'I do agree. But if at the end of the week, the kids raise more for charity by this absurd method, what does it matter?'

Baxter was silent. He began to sling books into his briefcase, then looked up disagreeably as Miss Peterson and Mr Sutcliffe came into the room, chuckling.

'What's so funny?' he demanded.

'Jenkins,' answered Miss Peterson.

'Oh, him. Silence broken in the first five minutes, no doubt.'

'On the contrary, maintained through the day, despite provocation.'

'From whom?' asked Miss Summers. 'No, let me guess . . .'

'That's right. Doyle. That young man is up to something, trying to trip up Jenkins and putting a lot of effort into it. But this time he met his match. Just read out that poem, Graham.'

Mr Sutcliffe obliged.

'Well, now,' said Miss Summers. 'One up to Peter. If he keeps it up for a week, I shall subscribe to his sheet myself.'

'Ah, you should have more faith, June. I've got my name down for 20p a day,' said Miss Peterson.

'A quid for a week's silence from Jenkins. That's a bargain,' admitted Baxter, grudgingly.

'All the same,' he added. 'I don't like the way this sponsored walk is folding up. It was a School Council proposal and now it looks like folding in favour of a scheme dreamed up by a young lady who's done all she can to give the Council a bad name.'

'What, Trisha?' said Miss Summers. 'That's a bit strong isn't it? No, I don't think you can put the blame on her, now. But,' she went on, 'I'm truly sorry for Penny Lewis. Her nose is properly out of joint – and some of the girls are being very unkind about it all.'

Sutcliffe nodded. 'Yes, poor old Penny.'

Chapter 14

While the staff were talking about Penny she was taking a short-cut home through the back streets, trying to walk off her irritation. All day she had been cheerful in a determined way, trying to encourage the smaller and smaller number of people who were on the sponsored walk. What made it worse was that some, who had gone over to the slurp-in seeing they were on a winner, had been plaguing the lives out of the remaining Walkers. Even since Miss Summers had closed the lists and no one could transfer, some were dropping out so as not to be left on the losing side.

'There aren't any winners or losers,' Penny told one group of girls. 'As long as we raise some money for charity.' They shrugged and walked away. As she came into the cloakroom at the end of the day she thought she heard someone say: 'The skids are under madam and about time too . . .' The voice tailed off as she came in. Someone giggled. But there was ill-feeling in the air. Some people wanted to see her put down. She shrugged, picked up her bag and walked out. Behind her the conversation started again, with shrieks of laughter.

Crossing the main street she walked quickly through the shopping centre – all lit up for Christmas. Ten days to go, she thought. She'd have a brood over the holiday and maybe next term pack in the School Council lark. She was on a beating to nothing. Suddenly, ahead of her, she saw Justin Bennett, walking slowly along. On impulse she hurried and caught up with him.

'Taking the short-cut home, Justin?'

He reddened slightly. 'In a way, yes.'

'Mind if I walk with you?'

He hesitated, then said: 'I have to call somewhere, it's a bit out of the way.'

'OK.' They walked along in silence. Penny determined to talk.

'I hear you have some mystery project for the Competition.'

'No mystery, really,' he answered. 'Just a bit unusual. I want to finish it before anyone else knows about it.'

'Sorry. I shouldn't have asked.'

'Doesn't matter, really.' He told her briefly about Mrs Carter and the Memory Scrapbook.

'It sounds great. Are you calling there now?'

'She's away. I'm just checking on things.'

They turned into Kettlewell Street and while she waited on the pavement, he climbed the stone steps to Mrs Carter's front door.

'Won't be a minute. I just have to put something out for the cat.'

Soon he was back again, hurrying down the steps to check a small door beneath them. He pointed.

'This is where she keeps her wheelchair.'

'Do you see her every day?'

'Well, most days.'

'Fantastic. And you kept it all to yourself. You are funny, Justin.'

'I don't see.'

'I didn't mean it that way,' she added hastily. 'I think it's great, but keeping it to yourself.'

He shrugged: 'I find it easier keeping things to myself sometimes.' He paused, and looked at her. 'I sometimes envy you the way you get on with everybody. This School Council bit.'

She laughed. 'Well you can see where it's landed me — right in the semolina. To tell the truth, coming along now, I was thinking of packing it in.'

'I wouldn't do that,' he said quickly.

She stared. He looked embarrassed, then went on:

'It sounds funny. But, you know, my parents — that is my father — thinks I don't fit in at Grange Hill. He thinks I'm wasting my time and ought to transfer to the High School. Then I'd be less — out of place.'

'Oh lord,' said Penny. 'They sent my brother there. Very stiff upper lip. But not me. They don't mind my being at Grange Hill. They don't seem to mind what I do. I wish they did sometimes. But, do you want to change?'

He shook his head. 'I do feel out of place at Grange Hill, in a way. You are, too, in a way, aren't you? But you like it. Well, I like it too, it's alive.' He paused: 'Mrs Carter said "they'll have to carry me out of Grange Hill". I feel a bit like that. I've put a lot into getting used to the School. Why should I leave, now?'

She grinned: 'Right on.'

They walked on in silence till they reached the corner of her road. They stood a moment, shifting their feet to keep warm in the chill air.

'You had a rough time today, Penny. I think the trouble is that,' he hesitated, 'you get up the noses of some people.'

'Like?'

'Like Trisha Yates. You irritate her. You seem to have it all going for you.'

'If only she knew. I envy her.'

He stared: 'You envy Trisha Yates?'

'Oh yes. I have to think about things so much. If she thinks something's right or wrong, she says so, right out.

56

I couldn't have done what she did over that school uni-form protest. I'd like to get on with her. I'd like to talk to her more. In fact I nearly did today.'

'What, about semolina?'

'No, about her friend, Cathy. She's in some sort of trouble. I'm quite sure she is. Only Trisha's so taken up with this slurp business, she doesn't seem to notice.'

'Perhaps you ought to talk to her.'

'Perhaps. I'll think about it. See you, Justin.'

'See you, Penny.'

Chapter 15

Cathy Hargreaves sat in one of the swings on the recreation ground and shivered. It was cold and barely light. She ought to go home. But she'd missed Neil that lunchtime and had come here on the off chance. The trouble was that she didn't know where he lived. She didn't even know his second name. It was stupid. They'd only met three times altogether. But she felt she'd known him for ages. She idly pushed with her foot and set the swing going, to and fro, lost in thought.

Without warning, there was a violent push on the seat of the swing. 'Get off!' she yelled angrily as she shot forward, grabbing wildly for the chains to hold on to her place. She tried to twist round and stop the sudden rush backwards, but as she did, another brutal push sent her flying. She lost grip, fell from the seat and sprawled on the ground. As she struggled up, she was pushed down again. She knew before she looked up in the half light, who it was. The two of them were leaning on the swing frame, the big one with his cropped hair and flat nose, grinning at her, the other one, small, pimply-faced, half-closed eyes.

'Oh dear, did we have a tumble? What a pity that nice little boy isn't here to pick us up.'

She scrambled up and moved to walk away. The big one who had spoken headed her off, blocking her way with his arm, one fist resting on the iron support of the swing frame.

'Perhaps he's been frightened off.'

Cathy felt a new twinge of fear.

'You don't even know who he is.'

'Oh yes, we do. We've been watching you. Saw you in the shelter yesterday, when you thought nobody was watching. Bad girl. Do your parents know you do that with your boy friend?'

'You lying –' Cathy screamed. She was suddenly angry and stepped towards him. He put his hands up in mock panic.

'Knock it off.' The other lad had spoken, quietly, through his teeth. Cathy's tormenter was silent.

'Hello, Cathy.'

Madelin was there, a few yards away, her white trouser suit showing in the dusk.

'Take no notice of him, Cathy. Small things amuse small minds.' Madelin came closer. 'Look, it's getting dark. You ought to be home by now. We won't keep you a minute.'

'What do you want?' asked Cathy.

'That favour you were going to do me, to make up for last year.'

'I never said I'd do you any favour, Madelin.'

'I know. I said you would.' Madelin's voice was hard. 'Listen. My friends are going to rob your place. But they don't like making a mess. So they won't break in.'

Cathy stared unbelievingly. Madelin went on.

'What you have to do is make sure your dad forgets to lock those fancy new patio doors you've got. Don't look so stupid. We've looked your place over from the outside. We just want a little peep inside. My friends are very smart. The Old Bill's very annoyed with them. It's "no visible means of entry" all the time. That's because we have lots of willing little helpers.'

'You won't get this one,' said Cathy, loudly.

'Nasty temper. Don't you shout at me, Cathy Hargreaves. You're going to help us.'

'I'm not.'

The pimply-faced lad spoke quietly. Unknown to Cathy he now stood just behind her.

'We'll rub your boy friend's face up a brick wall.'

Cathy felt sick. She swallowed.

'I'll tell the police.'

'What will you tell them? That you came all the way over here and nasty Madelin Tanner threatened you. What are they going to say? They'll remember that little business last year.' Madelin sneered. 'Now you know what it's like to have a little bit of form. No one believes a blind word you say.' Her voice was bitter.

'You do us this favour, and that's your lot. You don't, and your troubles'll start. First your boy friend. He's not very strong. My friend here could make a . . .'

Cathy snatched her bag from the ground and ran. No one stopped her. But Madelin called.

'We'll be in touch. Don't worry. And don't tell anyone. We'll get to him first.'

Cathy ran down the long road towards Brookdale. It was not far, but it seemed to take an age. The cold air burnt her throat and her chest ached. The streets by the school were deserted. But two third year girls hung round the gate. They stared at her as she ran up, breathless, barely able to speak.

'I want to find Neil.'

'Neil who?'

'I don't know his second name, he's . . .'

One of them looked more closely at her.

'You're from Grange Hill, aren't you?'

Cathy didn't answer. They moved towards her. She

60

moved off. They did not follow her, but one shouted:

'You keep clear of this place. Or else.'

On her own in the dark street, Cathy turned and began to walk home. What was she going to do?

Chapter 16

Cathy's misery went unnoticed in school next day. The place was full of excitement from the morning on. The list on the notice board had closed at: Slurp-in 100; Walk 20; Silence 2.

But the excitement reached a peak in the afternoon as Doyle put Plan A into operation with devastating effect. It began first thing as Tucker bowled into the classroom. After the stunning success of his poem yesterday, he was ready for a day's silent warfare with Doyle. And he had some tricks up his sleeve. Watch it, Doyly.

But, as Tucker entered, Doyle ignored him. He and his mates were busy in one corner of the room with a crowd round them. They were talking about the election for the new parents' committee. Robo's dad was a candidate, it seemed, and Robo had become a politician overnight.

' 'Course, if my dad gets elected, he'll tell Llewellyn a thing or two about these new timetables and things in the school.'

'Get off,' said one lad. 'What for?'

'Well, look at the way he's mucked the forms up, shifting everybody round.' Someone laughed and Robo got bolder.

'There's more chocos around here than a box of Black Magic.'

Tucker eyed them. Benny Green, he noticed, was looking out of the window as if he hadn't heard. But Doyle was half-looking at him, waiting for him to say something. It was a set up. Tucker went to his desk and noisily began laying books out.

Then Doyle spoke. Tucker knew it was meant for him.

'Come on, Robo. Your dad's bound to get elected. There are two places for this year and two standing, your dad and Bennett's mother. There won't be a vote unless some idiot puts up another name.'

'Well, anyway,' answered Robo, 'if they had a vote, my dad'd win.'

He went on: 'Who's going to vote for Bennett's old woman anyway – the snobs and the WIGS.'

'What's WIGS?' asked one lad, innocently.

'West Indian gentleman, didn't you know?'

Tucker looked round. He caught Hughes's eye, then Doyle's.

Doyle said: 'Were you going to say something, Mr Jenkins?'

Miss Peterson breezed in. Doyle always timed things well.

'Good morning, troops.'

'Good morning, miss.'

'Trisha. You have an announcement, I believe.'

Trisha Yates came to the front. Tucker glared at her. Pongo was getting a bit over the odds, lately.

'I just want to announce two things. The first is the semolina list is closed. No one, but no one, gets on now. If we last out the week, we raise nearly £200 and then this firm's going to double that. And if we go a second week, the school's been told, *Nationwide* might send a camera crew down.'

'Quiet, quiet!' shouted Miss Peterson amid the din of talking and laughing. 'Things are going very well. Let's keep it that way. Meanwhile, another two weeks to go before term end. We have work to do. It's not all semolina and silence. So eyes down, look in.'

The morning passed. Doyle seemed to be holding his hand and apart from some whispered remarks gave no more trouble. Yet Tucker had a feeling something was brewing. They were out to get him. He'd have liked to chat it over with Benny. But Benny went off with Alan at lunch-time, to sit on the semolina tables where the noise and the stupid jokes about TV were deafening. Tucker shrugged and ate on his own. After lunch break he went back to the classroom, ready for anything. But when it came, it took him by surprise.

It happened in the last period. Miss Peterson was in charge and she allowed them to work on their Competition Entries. Tucker thought of writing more verses to his poem, but he was too much on edge. Ten minutes before time, Miss Peterson looked up.

'Now you lot, keep at it. I have to go out for a few minutes. I count on you to carry on, quietly. Follow Peter's example. Absolute silence.'

Silence there was for two minutes. Then Doyle said quite distinctly.

'What was it you were saying about your brother, Macker?'

'He lost his newspaper round job,' answered Macker.

'Get off – how was that?'

'It was Snowball. He was trying to screw more money out of our kid, but he wasn't having any. So the little sod messed the papers up and got him the push. Bad enough his dad ripping off the Social, but he has to rip our kid's job off.'

Benny was on his feet.

'You're a liar, Macker.'

Macker was waiting for this. He stood up.

'What you going to do about it, golly?'

Tucker barely felt himself move. He left his desk and

reached Macker in one leap. Macker went down with a crash and Tucker was pounding his face, saying between each punch: 'I've-had-enough-of-you-today-Macker.'

'All right, all right, all right.'

In the doorway was Baxter. Tucker rolled off Macker and stood up. He knew in that second he was done for. Doyly had hung him out to dry.

'Quick march, Jenkins. Head's office for you.'

'Sir!' Benny was trying to say something.

'That'll do, Green. Come on, Jenkins.'

'Just a minute, Mr Baxter.'

Miss Peterson was there, barring the way.

'I'll handle this, thank you. Go to your seat, Jenkins. I'm sorry you were bothered with this, Mr Baxter. We'll sort it out.'

Baxter glared. He looked as though he'd speak, then changed his mind, and walked out.

'Right,' said Miss Peterson. 'The rest of you pack your rolls and head for home. Jenkins, stay behind.'

When the classroom was empty, Tucker stood defiantly by his desk.

'Miss. It was . . .'

Miss Peterson looked at him a second.

'I'm sure it was, Peter. I think I know what happened. I overheard the election meeting this morning. Loyalty to your friends is your great quality, Peter. But you have got to learn how to keep control and not to be provoked.'

He pursed his lips.

'Apart from anything, you've blown your silence for today.'

Tucker made a face.

'I'm packing that in, miss.'

'Ah,' said Miss Peterson. 'A pity. That's one up for the opposition.'

Chapter 17

Baxter and Miss Peterson confronted one another in the staffroom. Miss Summers and Sutcliffe watched from their chairs. Both of them spoke quietly, but the air was tense.

'I was just down the corridor when you moved in,' said Miss Peterson.

'There was a riot.'

'There was a scuffle.'

'Big scuffle.'

'A scuffle,' insisted Miss Peterson. 'And you had no right to run Jenkins off to the boss without telling me.'

Baxter glared, then nodded.

'OK. But Jenkins is asking for it.'

Miss Peterson shook her head. 'Jenkins is being set up. Someone knows one false move and he's for the chop.'

'Who's this?' asked Miss Summers.

'Doyle is trying to provoke Jenkins into doing something stupid.'

Miss Summers opened her eyes wider. 'But I thought Doyle was a model of good behaviour just now. All that help he gave Trisha Yates with the semolina slurp – local newspaper reports, arranging the rules, and so on.'

'Doyle is hatching his own scheme for his own ends.'

'Ah yes,' put in Sutcliffe. 'Like father, like son. Mr Doyle is up to something with this new parents' advisory. I'm convinced of it.'

Miss Peterson nodded. 'I think so. There was an election meeting going on in the form today.' She told them briefly what she had overheard.

'Oh,' said Baxter, 'so you reckon Mr Doyle is out to put a cracker under the boss's nice new form arrangements. I thought his party were all for sweetness and light.'

'Hm,' said Miss Peterson. 'I think what we're dealing with is Doyle's private army.'

'Too right,' said Sutcliffe. 'That's the one party he's interested in – The Doyle Benefit Society.'

'Graham!' Baxter sounded shocked: 'What a way to speak of our respected Chairman of Governors.'

'To be honest,' said Sutcliffe, 'I'd trust him as far as I could throw him, and Doyle junior a little less.'

'Tut, tut. The child can only live up to your expectations.'

'I'm afraid he'll do just that,' answered Sutcliffe.

'The thing that worries me,' said Miss Peterson, packing her bag, 'is that Peter Jenkins will live up to expectations. That could be disastrous.'

Chapter 18

Unable to believe his luck, Tucker charged out of school and was down by the main road before he realized that Alan, Hughes and Benny were waiting for him. He pulled up sharp and they crowded round.

'What happened?'

He told them.

'Old Miss Peterson sussed Doyly out, OK,' said Hughes. 'I thought you were for the chop.' Alan thumped him on the back. 'You were lucky, Tucker. But what about the Big Hush? – you blew that.'

'Dah,' said Tucker, waving his hand. 'That's finished. Two days of it creased me.' He looked at Benny. Benny still wasn't talking.

Alan chuckled. 'I thought you'd destroy Macker. You got him off balance. He's bigger.'

'Right,' said Hughes. 'Hey, Tucker. You reckon they'll wait and jump you?'

'Tell you what,' said Alan. 'We walk home your way. Then if they start on you, they get the package deal, eh?'

Tucker grinned. They crossed the road. 'Changing the subject,' he said, 'where's Flash Harry tonight?'

They looked round. The familiar car was nowhere to be seen.

'Come on, fellers.' Tucker led the way through the side streets. 'I feel like doing something totally stupid to-night.'

'So, what's the difference?' asked Alan.

'Follow me, subjects,' said Tucker, for he had had a sudden brilliant idea. As they came into Broadwood Road, work was in full swing on the site. The gate was empty, but as luck would have it, on the level ground, by the mesh fence, stood the dumper, massive and red.

'What d'you reckon to that, fellers. Our kid drives that.'

'Magic,' said Hughes. 'So?'

'Like a ride?' asked Tucker, rashly.

The others stared.

'How?'

'Meet us back here after tea. Like, seven-thirty.'

'How'll we get in?'

'Leave it to me.'

'How'll you start it?'

'Uncle Tucker'll fix everything.'

In the forecourt of Tucker's flats, Hughes and Alan peeled off. Benny, still silent, hung on. Tucker eyed him. Then Benny spoke.

'Dad says thanks for that note about the building job. He's going to look at it.' He laughed, embarrassed. 'Do you know what he said?'

Tucker shook his head.

'He says if he gets the job, I get more pocket money – if I don't do any more moonlighting.'

'Hey, he knew all the time,' said Tucker.

Benny shook his head: 'Nah. Mum knew. She wasn't saying 'cause she knew about that tool kit I wanted to buy.'

'Great,' said Tucker. 'See you seven-thirty, eh?'

'Right on,' said Benny.

Chapter 19

Det-con. Houston came down the police station steps, his mouth still full of tea leaves. Why did he always get the back end of the pot? That mob in there were always taking the mickey. Bunch of flats. He climbed into his old car. He was off duty, but he'd have a cruise round first. You never knew, and a good copper was always on duty.

He drove down to the shopping centre, cased it slowly, then turned into the back street. In Kettlewell Road he paused a while opposite the old house where he'd seen the Bennett lad messing about. No sign of him today. Still, keep him on file. You never knew. He swung out of Kettlewell, doubled back and drove along the Parade. He hadn't seen that coloured lad, Green, for the past few mornings. Had the kid tumbled? Nor that other one, Jenkins. Ever since he'd caught him switching newspapers. They must both be lying low.

He took in another few side streets, then drove up Broadwood. The building site would take a bit of watching. He slipped his foot off the gas pedal and steered in to the pavement opposite. He was in luck. There were four of 'em, Green, Jenkins and two others, one black, one white, hanging round the fence, nudging and pointing. He rolled down the window to get a better look. An icy blast of air hit his face and he screwed up his eyes. When he opened them again the lads were away down the road. What now?

He drove back to the shopping centre and bought himself a modest take-away from the Chinese Chippy. He sat in the car with it keeping a careful eye on passers-by. But he must have dozed off for when he looked at his watch again, it was gone six. Starting the car, he made his way back to the corner pub near the building site. Inside he settled down at one end of the bar with a half of lager and a bag of crisps. From there he could see who was coming in and ask the landlord about them, casually.

The bar began filling up, one table was surrounded by blokes from the site. Half an hour later they were joined by a stocky, grey-haired, sour-looking man, whom they greeted like a long-lost brother.

'If it isn't Mr Garfield. Come and rest your weary limbs. Will you have the usual?'

'You're a gent, Paddy,' Garfield replied and squeezed in among the crowd while Paddy brought over his pint.

'Now then, how's life in education?'

Garfield made a noise of disgust.

'If I could retire, I'd do it tomorrow, mate. Little b – '

'Now then,' called the landlord, cheerfully. 'Less of that. This is a respectable house.'

'Listen, mate,' answered Garfield. 'You can talk. You don't have to work there. A thousand of 'em. Why, I'd sooner work in the zoo – quieter – and better habits.'

'Ah, come on,' laughed Paddy. ' 'Tisn't so bad. There are some fine young people there. Just high spirits.'

Garfield glared at him. 'High spirits? Do you know what they're doing now?' He raised his voice. 'Eating semolina every day for charity.'

The table rocked. 'I don't believe you,' said Paddy.

'Look at the local rag, then.' Garfield dragged it out of his pocket. 'Slurp-in goes from strength to strength,' he read. 'Slurp-in! It's all on our taxes, mate. That's modern education!'

'But it's for charity, man. Have a heart.'

71

Garfield finished his pint. 'You don't have to work there,' he repeated. He looked round. Houston stepped forward. 'Let me buy you a drink, Mr Garfield,' he said.

Garfield looked at him. 'Thanks. Do I know you?'

'No,' said Houston hastily, passing the glass to the landlord. 'I just happened to hear you talking about the school.' He handed the full glass back to Garfield and eased his chair closer.

'Oh yes,' said Garfield. 'What about it?'

'You were talking about some of the things the pupils get up to. I find that very interesting.'

Paddy and his mates rose.

'On our way,' said Paddy, saluting the landlord. As he passed he nudged Garfield and made a sign which Houston did not see. Garfield took a long swig at his beer and turned to Houston, eyeing him closely.

'What was that you were saying?'

'About the pupils at Grange Hill?' Houston asked encouragingly.

Garfield downed a third of his pint at one gulp, looked at the landlord then turned to Houston.

'Pupils? Oh, I never discuss school business out of hours. As much as my job is worth.'

He drained his glass, and slapped it on the table. On his feet he turned again to Houston.

'Have to get back to school. Evening classes tonight. Thanks for the drink.'

'Any time,' said Houston, gloomily.

Chapter 20

At eight o'clock, Houston felt he'd had enough of his
fellow men. He finished his drink, said good night to the
landlord and went to find his car, parked opposite the
building site.

As he reached the car, the evening air was split by a
gigantic roar like a tank engine. Houston jumped like a
shot rabbit. He about-faced. It came from the building
site, now in darkness. Behind the metal fence, a light
flashed and a giant shadow moved with a crunching sound.
Houston started into the road. He could hardly believe his
eyes. Someone was driving a flipping dumper round in
circles in the open space beyond the fence. From the
shouts and laughter it was clear it was no site worker
on overtime. Those lads, he remembered them from earlier
that evening. Got 'em bang to rights.

He charged across the road, shouting, but the merry
crew on the dumper did not hear him, or took no notice.
He struggled to pull his notebook out of his pocket as he
reached the open slope below the gate. But as he arrived,
a bright light shone from behind him, catching the dumper
in its beam as the truck ran alongside the gate for the
third time.

Houston swivelled round. A little invalid car had driven
right up on the slope beside him and a broad-shouldered
black man was struggling to get out of the tiny door.
Pulling himself upright, the man roared: 'Tucker! Benny!
You others! Come off there and double quick.'

In that instant the lights on the dumper went out. The

engine stopped. There was a mad scramble from the vehicle.

'No use you running off. I know you're there,' bellowed the black man. 'Get yourselves over here.'

Four figures came from the darkness and stood sheepishly by the fence.

'Now you listen to me,' he went on, still at the top of his voice. 'If you four put together had the brains God gave a rabbit, you'd know even grown men get killed on waggons like that. You, Benny, how d'you think I got my back broke? And I wasn't playing around, man. I was doing my job. If that dumper turned over, we'd be scraping you lot off the ground.'

The boys stood silent. Mr Green paused for breath.

'Just a moment,' said Houston, who felt it was time to take over. 'I'd better have these lads' names. Then we'll see their parents.'

The big man looked at Houston, resting his hand on the little car roof. He eyed the detective up and down.

'I shouldn't worry about that, sir. I'm in charge here.'

'In charge?' asked Houston.

'Yes, sir. I'm the gateman for all Billington building sites. Don't you worry. I'll see the boys' parents. Don't you worry.' He stared Houston down.

'If you're sure.'

'Of course I'm sure, sir. Don't I sound sure, or something?' The black man loomed over Houston and for a second he felt intimidated.

'Very well,' he said awkwardly. 'As long as you're in charge.'

When he was gone, Mr Green called to the lads.

'I don't know how you got in but shift yourselves out and quick. And if I catch any of you in here again, I'll skin you and that's not advertising.'

Five minutes later the boys stood in front of him. He glared at them, then decided to say no more.

'Hey, Dad,' Benny said, in a small voice. 'Are you really gateman?'

'I go for the interview tomorrow. Now you get home and quick.'

Chapter 21

By morning the news was all over Grange Hill School. Tucker's parents, Alan's and Hughes's had nominated Benny's dad for the parents' committee. The excitement built up rapidly. Doyle came into the classroom in the morning to find a large poster 'Vote for Green', on the wall.

At first he was taken aback. But he soon recovered. He turned to his side-kick, Robo. 'I don't suppose anybody'll vote for a bloke who's not working and on the Social.'

Tucker rounded on Doyle.

'What d'you mean? Benny's dad's done more days' hard graft than Robo's dad's had hot dinners.'

At break time, posters with 'Green for King', and 'Sam Green rules, OK', appeared on the railings. Tucker and his mates started a march round the yard, chanting and singing.

By lunch-time, Doyle decided things had gone far enough. As Justin Bennett came out of the dining-hall he was seized by Robo and Macker and hustled over to a quiet corner of the yard. Justin was scared but he tried not to show it.

'What do you lot want?' he asked.

'Listen,' said Doyle, reasonably. 'This parents' election. You know they've put up Benny Green's dad.'

'Yes,' answered Justin. 'What's wrong with that?'

'We don't want a nig nog putting up,' said Macker impatiently. Doyle shoved his elbow in Macker's ribs.

'Shut up, will you,' he said. 'Look, Justin. If three people put up, one's going to be beaten. The vote'll be split.'

'I can see that,' said Justin doubtfully.

'So, why can't your old lady drop out?' butted in Robo.

Justin looked at him.

'Even if I asked her to, she wouldn't. And I wouldn't ask her anyway.'

'Why not?'

'Because I think you're a lot of cruds.'

It took some saying, but he got it out. Just as they closed in on him, someone spoke up behind them.

'Hello, hello, hello. What's all this?'

The group split apart. There was Tucker, Alan, Benny, Hughes and a dozen other lads.

'What's this? Intimidation?' said Tucker. He poked his finger several times into Doyle's chest: 'You-leave-Justin-Bennett-alone-Get it?'

Doyle and his troop, outnumbered, withdrew to another part of the yard. Ten minutes later another march started. This time the posters said: 'Green-Bennett in; Robinson out'.

Doyle watched them march by, biting his lip. It was clearly time for strong measures. He decided to put Plan B into operation.

Chapter 22

On the afternoon of semolina day 4, something funny happened. Correction: something peculiar happened. Some thought it was a giggle. But others didn't find it funny at all.

After lunch several pupils in each class had to leave the room. That might not have been strange, maybe the lessons were boring. But they all left at once. One teacher thought his lot were putting him on and tried to stop them, but they all rushed out, looking desperate. And they all came back looking pale and weak. It was a bad dose of the old Costa del Sols and no mistake.

Before she left school that day, Trisha was cornered in the cloaks by half a dozen girls. She looked at them suspiciously.

'What's up with you lot?'

'We're packing this Semolina lark in, that's what.'

'Oh, come on. The week's up tomorrow. Can't you last out?'

'You're joking. I'm not spending Friday afternoon on the loo,' said one.

Trisha stared. 'You're off your wheels. Semolina's nothing to do with that. It's some bug.'

'That's your story,' came the answer.

Next day there were twenty missing from the semolina tables and Trisha watched them like an anxious mother. It didn't make any difference. That afternoon there was a mass walk-out – twenty in one form, fifteen in another. Trisha was in despair.

At break time, she saw Tucker and Benny Green laughing round the notice board in the corridor. Someone had put up a notice.

'Why bother with a Sponsored Walk? A Sponsored
Run is Quicker. Semolina reaches the parts other
muck can't reach.'

She pushed through and tore down the paper. It was made up of letters cut from newspapers. Someone was making sure they were not found out. She rounded on Tucker.

'You think that's funny?'

'As a matter of fact I do – that's why I'm laughing.'

She raged at him: 'You rotten . . .'

'Hey,' said Tucker. 'Don't go spare at me. I didn't put it up.'

'Yeah? That's your story.' She pushed out of the group and walked away.

Worse was to come. During the last period, she was called into the Head's office. Mr Llewellyn had Matron with him. He looked serious.

'Trisha. I'm afraid the semolina sessions have to stop.'

'Sir,' she protested. 'There's no proof it's that that's making people ill.'

Matron intervened:

'I'm afraid, Trisha, that all the people who had upsets were semolina people. No one else had trouble.'

Mr Llewellyn shook his head. 'We shall have to suspend the operation, Trisha. Still, you completed one week and I'm sure the sponsors won't let you down.'

'But we were going on for a second week, with *Nationwide* and all . . .'

'Goodness me, no, Trisha. Imagine if the TV cameras

came down and we had all 80 of you ill. Our toilets couldn't cope. There'd be a scandal.'

Trisha knew he was right. She turned to go. The Head stopped her.

'Just between you and I, do you think that someone can be sabotaging your efforts?'

Her eyes grew round.

'How, sir? You mean putting something in the semolina?'

'It sounds incredible – how did they do it for one thing? But it's not impossible, you know,' said Mr Llewellyn. 'We'll make some discreet enquiries. If I find out someone was responsible, Trisha, rest assured I shall jump upon them from a very great height.'

As Trisha came back into the class the room was quiet. Mr Sutcliffe looked up from his desk.

'Well, Trish?'

'Mr Llewellyn says we have to call it off, sir.'

There was uproar for a moment, shouts of 'Shame', answered by louder shouts of 'Great' and 'About time'. Mr Sutcliffe silenced them.

'I'm very sorry, Trisha. You worked very hard. You didn't deserve such bad luck.'

As she went back to her seat, Doyle whispered loudly:

'Well, I reckon that semolina was doctored. Someone slipped something in. I wonder who'd do a cruddy thing like that.'

'That's enough, Michael,' commanded Mr Sutcliffe.

When lessons finished, Trisha went to the cloaks. It was full of chattering girls. But everyone stopped talking the moment she came in. She picked up her bags and left. Someone said loudly: 'I had two days of flipping agony because of her stupid idea. Should have called it off right away.'

For a second Trisha thought of storming back in there, but changed her mind and walked out of school. As she neared the gate she saw Penny standing in her path.

'Trisha. I'd like a word with you,' she said.

'Not you as well,' answered Trisha abruptly. 'No, I'm off home.' She swerved round Penny and ran through the gates.

Chapter 23

Trisha arrived home to find Mum in the kitchen drinking tea with Carol. Both greeted her with broad smiles. She guessed from their faces they'd just been having a giggle and thought she knew why.

'I suppose you think it's very funny,' she snapped.

Her sister smiled.

'Well, you must admit it has a funny side.'

'If you'd put as much into organizing this as I have, you wouldn't think it so bloody funny.'

'Mind your language, Trisha Yates,' said her mother.

'I don't care.' Trisha's voice rose. 'It's not funny!' She flung her bag in the corner, tore off her coat and rushed upstairs. She'd have loved to break a kitchen chair over her sister's head. Safe in her room she sat on her bed, breathing deeply. Why did people have to mess up everything you tried to do?

There was a knock on the door.

'Piglet.'

It was Carol.

'Can I come in?'

'Get lost.'

'Listen, Trish. I'm sorry. I thought it was a giggle. I didn't know you'd be upset. I'm sorry.'

The door opened. Carol peeped through.

'Honest. I know you worked hard on that semolina lark. But it began as a joke and I thought it ended that way.'

She came in, sat on the bed and put her arm round

Trisha's shoulder. 'Come on, Piglet. It's not the end of the world. Just the end of the week. You lasted out, or most of you. You've raised hundreds of quid for charity. What more would you do?'

Trisha bit her lip.

'I know. But we were going to have a second week and raise more with TV and all. But,' she stood up from the bed and faced her sister, 'what makes it worse is that it looks as though some pig sabotaged the whole thing.'

Carol put her hand to her mouth and kept her face straight:

'You mean, dosed the semolina?'

Trisha nodded.

'Yes, that was rotten,' said Carol. 'Could have made someone really ill.'

Trisha walked over to the window and looked out.

'Then to put the lid on it, who should come up to me in that sickening way of hers, and try to be nice, but Penny flipping Templeton Lewis.'

Carol raised her eyebrows.

'That lady gets you, doesn't she?'

Trisha didn't answer. Carol beckoned her back to the bed.

'Sit down, Trish. You know, it's not her, it's you. Look, I know she's too smart and too cool. And she gets up your nose. So what? That's how they make 'em where she comes from. You're you and what's wrong with that?'

'What's that got to do with it?'

'Listen, Piglet. If you thought, you'd know you're as good as she is. Our family's as good as theirs any day. So what does it matter what she's like. I mean, has she actually done you a bad turn?'

Trisha shook her head.

'Well, then. If you don't like her, leave her. But don't let her get to you. She's a girl, nothing more. Listen, kid, when I started there were even more like her in my class. Some of them right little madams. I didn't like 'em. Couldn't stand 'em. When I worked it out, I realized it was because they seemed to find life so easy. It was all a bowl of cherries to them. They were so successful, it made me sick.'

'So?' Trisha was interested, though she wouldn't show it.

'I was sure they were looking down on me. Some of 'em were. But the trouble was I was looking up to them and hating it at the same time. And there was no reason to look up to them. Who were they anyway? So I washed it all out. I got to like some of them. Some were still real bitches. But they couldn't get to me any more.'

Carol paused, grinned at her sister.

'That was a lecture. Come on, let's have a cup of tea. It'll be all better tomorrow.'

'Trisha!' Her mother called from downstairs.

Carol opened the door. 'What is it, Mum?'

'Someone to see Trisha. Penny Lewis.'

Chapter 24

When Trisha got down to the kitchen, Penny was seated at the table and Mum was making another pot of tea.

'Hello.'

'Hello.'

They were both awkward.

'Look, love,' said Mum. 'There's tea in the pot. Carol and I'll go next door, so you can have a chat in peace.'

Penny and Trisha looked at one another over the tea cups. Trisha spoke first.

'Sorry I was narky at you just now.'

Penny smiled: 'It doesn't matter. If I were in your place, I'd be rolling over and biting the carpet in a rage. After all your work. It was rotten.'

Trisha made a face.

'I should have said that to you, earlier in the week. First your sponsored walk went for a burton, then my sponsored run.'

They both laughed. Trisha felt easier.

'Still we've raised some money for charity. Maybe some of our people can come on the walk, if we can fix it up. If you like I'll put my name down.'

Penny smiled.

'That's generous of you, Trisha. I wish I could be like that. If I have to change my mind, it takes me ages and I try and keep quiet about it. I wish I could speak out like you do.'

'Oh me,' grinned Trisha. 'No sooner think than speak and usually speak first, that's what Mum says.'

There was a silence.

'Trisha. I'm glad we had our chat. But I really came here to talk about something else.'

'What's that?'

'Cathy Hargreaves.'

'Oh, Cathy.' Trisha felt guilty suddenly.

'I think she's in trouble.'

'Eh? What sort?'

'Yes. You know she's been slipping over Brookdale way at lunch-time and so on.'

Trisha nodded. 'I had noticed. I didn't say anything. I've been busy and anyway, if she's seeing a feller, it's not my business.'

'I think there's something more. The other night I saw her with Madelin Tanner.'

'I don't believe it!'

'I didn't, Trisha, but it's true. They were standing in the light by the zebra at the shopping centre. Madelin looked – well – she looked nasty. And both of them looked as though they'd been having a real heart to heart.'

'Cathy's parents'll kill her if they find out.'

'I know. But why should she want to? Madelin got her into real trouble.'

'I don't know. Look, Penny, have you got five minutes?'

'Yes?'

'Well can you come round with me to Cathy's? We'll get her to come out for a coffee. Tell her it's important school business. Then, we'll ask her.'

'Will she talk?'

'Oh, she'll trust me. I've never split on her.'

'All right.'

Penny picked up her bag. Trisha put her coat on again and called through to her mother.

Then the two of them set off through the streets to

Cathy's home, walking swiftly for the evening air was chill. At Cathy's front door they rang and waited, stamping their feet to keep warm. The door flew open. Cathy stood in front of them, pale-faced and wide-eyed.

'Cathy, can you come out for a quick coffee? We just want a word.'

She shook her head. 'I'm doing something for Mum.'

Trisha felt Cathy was not telling the truth. She beckoned Cathy on to the step. She pulled the door behind her.

'Listen, Cathy. It's important. We think you need a bit of help.'

'Help?' Cathy was aggressive. 'What d'you mean?'

She glared at Penny as much as to say 'What do *you* want?'

Penny said: 'Cathy, it's about Madelin Tanner.'

'Her.' Cathy's lips tightened. 'Haven't seen her since last year.'

'But . . .' said Penny.

'Madelin Tanner's nothing to do with me,' Cathy insisted. She opened the front door and stepped inside.

'Look, Mum's waiting for me.'

'Cathy,' said Trisha. 'Let's have a talk at school on Monday?'

'OK,' said Cathy from inside the door. 'If you're not too busy.'

Penny and Trisha looked at one another. The door banged shut and they were `eft outside.

'I'd better get home,' said Penny. 'But there is something wrong.'

'Too right, there is,' said Trisha. 'But what?'

Chapter 25

Cathy went from the front door straight up to her room and lay miserably on her bed until mid-evening. When she came down, her mother and brother Gary were watching television.

'What's up, Cathy, dear? You're looking poorly.'

'Oh, I'm all right, Mum,' she answered.

'No, you're not. I'll take you to the doctor's tomorrow.'

'Oh, no, Mum. There's nothing wrong. And surgery's always packed on Saturdays.'

Gary made a joke of it: 'You've been eating this semolina stuff, haven't you? One of the blokes was telling me his brother was on the go all yesterday with it.'

'Wouldn't touch that muck,' said Cathy.

'But, love, I thought it was your big friend Trisha who was running that semolina thing at school.' Cathy's mother looked closely at her. 'That's it. You've quarrelled with Trisha. Come on, tell us about it.'

'Oh, do leave off, Mum.'

'That's no way to talk.'

'Well, leave me alone then.' Cathy slammed out of the room, leaving them staring at one another.

She passed a miserable weekend, half afraid, half worried, but unable to decide what to do. Part of her wanted to go and search the streets till she found Neil. Part of her was afraid to venture out in case she met Madelin and her 'friends' again. The little one gave her the shudders.

On the Sunday she conquered her fear enough to get her coat on as though to go for a walk. But then came the sudden fear – suppose they followed her and found out where Neil lived. They reckoned to know him, but suppose that was a bluff?

Suppose she led them to him. Anxious one moment, afraid the next, she ended by taking off her coat and going back up to her room.

Later that evening, the phone rang. Her brother went to answer it but Cathy got there first. Perhaps Neil had found out where she lived and was getting in touch. She snatched up the phone.

'Hello, Cathy, dear.'

It was Madelin.

'You have been a good girl. Not a word to anyone. Very sensible. Now listen, Cathy. Tomorrow night you can do us that favour. Tomorrow night, Monday. Got it? Just make sure the catch is off. That's all you have to do.'

The phone went dead.

'Who was that?' asked Gary.

'I don't know,' said Cathy. 'Someone going on about something I couldn't understand. Wrong number.'

'Look, love,' said her mother. 'You have an early night tonight. You want to be fit for school. You've been like a lost soul all weekend.'

Cathy agreed silently. She knew she wouldn't be able to sleep. But she got undressed, washed and lay in bed looking at magazines until she heard her mother come upstairs. Then she switched off the light and lay in darkness, trying over and over again to sort out her thoughts. She heard the clock strike twelve and then one.

Suddenly she made up her mind what to do, turned round and, with a great effort, went off to sleep.

Chapter 26

Cathy was downstairs just after seven next morning. Her mother stared at her. She greeted her bravely.

'I thought I'd walk to school through the park and get some exercise,' she said.

'Get away, girl,' said her mother. 'It's freezing cold, and foggy.'

'I'll put an extra jumper and scarf on,' she answered and begar making herself some toast. Her mother eyed her but said nothing.

By eight o'clock she was out of the house and hurrying down the road. The cold air caught at her face and hurt her throat. But the fog was not too thick. She could see to the end of the road, though every now and then a breeze would lift the fog and show the houses farther ahead. In twenty minutes she reached the main road, half ran through the shopping centre and into the streets beyond. Here and there cars were coughing and snarling as their owners tried to start them. Cathy hurried on, following the road she'd seen Neil take that first night. As she walked she looked left and right and now and then glanced back. She saw nothing to alarm her yet. The road ended in a T-junction. Guessing, she turned left.

There was a phone box on the corner. Was that where Neil phoned to get the doctor for his sick sister? She stopped at a tiny row of terraced houses. An old man was at one front door. He stared and shook his head as Cathy asked him.

'He's as deaf as a post,' a woman called down the passage inside the house. 'What is it you want?'

'Please, do you know a boy called Neil. About 12, curly hair.'

'Only pensioners along here. Who else'd live in a dump like this? Try the new flats at the end.'

As Cathy walked swiftly along the pavement a car engine started behind her. She turned. Farther down the road, just visible in the fog was a small blue van. She passed the telephone box on the corner and came into an open space littered with bricks and rubble. At the back of it rose blocks of flats, raw and new. In front of them a man was starting his car. He shook his head at her question.

'New here,' he called as he drove off.

She went to the caretaker's flat on the ground floor and hammered at the door. No one came. She looked round. The blue van had left the road and was parked across the open space. She was sure she was being followed. The door was snatched open. A woman in a dressing-gown glared at her.

'Neil?' She made a face. 'I don't know. There's a couple of boys on the second landing. They're mostly new here.' Then she shut the door. The van engine started. This time, Cathy saw, in panic, it was heading across the open space, bumping and lurching.

'Cathy!'

Someone called from above her. She looked up, heart beating fast. Neil was looking down from the balcony, pulling his jacket on.

'What are you doing here?' he asked.

She heard the van move closer.

'Hey, I'll come down,' he called.

'No!' But he had vanished.

She started to run towards the stair entrance but the

van had driven on to the paved area in front of her, brakes screeching. She saw Madelin looking out of the side window, then the rear door opened, the bigger lad leapt out and grabbed her so fiercely that she was almost jerked off her feet.

'Get back, Neil!' she screamed, as she was dragged inside, on to the van floor.

Her bag fell on to the ground, scattering books and paper. The van door slammed. A hand was clamped over her mouth as the vehicle pulled violently away across the waste ground.

As they crashed back on to the road, she heard Madelin yell.

'Hey, the little sod's gone to the phone box. Go and get him.'

Chapter 27

Neil heard Cathy's scream, saw her dragged away as he dashed out of the passage into the freezing air. A few yards away, her books lay scattered. Without thinking he began to gather them up.

'Cathy Hargreaves,' he read.

Then he put down the books and looked round him. The van raced away across the waste ground, rocking from side to side. A sick feeling gripped his stomach. What was going on? Who were they? Why did she shout for him to get back?

These thoughts were through his head in a split second, then he was running across the open space for the phone box. He saw the van crash on to the road and drive away, then put on speed and snatched open the kiosk door. But just as he tumbled inside and lifted the phone, the van did a U-turn and he heard it heading back. He put the phone to his ear. It whined at him. Out of order. Now the van had stopped and through the window he saw a big lad jump from it and run towards him.

Run, he told himself. Pulling open the door he staggered out. It was bitterly cold and he had not managed to get his jacket on before he came down. First he ran back towards the flats, then saw the bloke was cutting him off. He turned the other way, dodged into a side street, ran full tilt along it, turned again and came out in the street beyond. He knew that a quarter of a mile along towards the main road was a newsagent's with a pay phone. If he could reach that . . .

His breath came ragged now, his chest ached and his legs grew heavier. As he came level with the shops he heard a shout.

Stupidly he stopped and looked behind him. The big bloke was coming on fast. With an effort Neil put on speed again, crossed the road, rounded the corner and ran on towards the main road. Behind him he heard the crunch of metal-shod boots on the pavement. If he could keep going, the police station was on the main road. He dared not look back, but knew his pursuer was gaining.

Like a hunted rabbit he zigzagged across the road, stumbled down a side turning and hit the main road near the traffic lights just as the green light came on. He hurled himself over, hearing car brakes go on and drivers swear. He almost tripped in the road and reached the other side exhausted. He halted, heart going like a hammer, cold air burning in his lungs. There was the bloke, crossing the road between him and the police station.

Panicking, Neil leapt over a flower bed beyond the pavement, jumped a low wall and headed down a turning. Now the pavements were crowded with kids. He ran blindly, pushing and shoving, thinking only of getting away. Then he was in the middle of a crowd of them, exhausted. He couldn't run a yard more. A few yards away were school gates. He'd run through to Grange Hill.

'Hey,' he grabbed a lad, gasping, 'Cathy!'

'Get off,' the lad pushed him off: 'What you on about?'

'Cathy – Cathy.' He couldn't remember her second name. 'She's . . .'

They crowded round him, lads and girls, staring and pointing. 'Hey, he's a Brookdaler. What d'you want round here, kidder? You'll get eaten.'

'Cathy . . .'

Someone had him by the neck. A deeper voice spoke.

'Come on, Neil.'

His pursuer had pushed through the crowd.

He writhed in the grip, bit at the hand on his collar, broke away and was grabbed again. The kids around them scattered.

'Just a minute. What is this?'

A huge, bearded man, Neil knew he must be a teacher, stood there, hands on hips. Neil's captor spoke hastily.

'It's my brother, sir. Run off when he should go to school.'

'Which school?'

'Brookdale, sir.'

'Oh yes. He wants to come to Grange Hill, does he? Don't blame him.' The bearded man grinned. The bloke was dragging Neil away.

'No, sir,' Neil forced out the words. 'It's Cathy . . .'

'What's that?' came the puzzled question.

'Oh, just another of his stories, sir, he's always making them up.'

'No, sir,' shrieked Neil, 'it's Cathy.'

From behind the bearded teacher, two girls, one red-headed, one brown-haired, pushed their way through the crowd.

'Did you say Cathy?' asked the red-head.

Neil nodded and tried to break loose. His captor gripped viciously on his neck and lifted him off his feet. But the brown-haired girl sprang forward and held Neil by his jumper.

'D'you mean Cathy Hargreaves?'

'Yes, they've got her.'

The grip on his neck loosened. There was a crunch of boot metal as the bloke let go and ran.

'Just a minute, my lad,' grunted the bearded teacher. 'You hang on. What's this about Cathy Hargreaves? Hey!'

There was a scuffle, the thump of bone on flesh. Neil saw his tormentor fall to the ground. Then he knelt on the pavement and was sick.

Chapter 28

Det-con. Houston came into the station office and headed for the tea-pot. He'd spent an hour trying to find out from Billington's whether that bloke Green was their gateman. But as per usual, the people in charge didn't come into the office till mid-morning. He needed a cup of tea. To his surprise he'd caught PC Benson in the act of making a fresh pot. The uniformed man, what's more, greeted him pleasantly.

'Just in time, Brian. We've made an extra pot in cele-bration.'

'Of what?' asked Houston, suspiciously.

'Sergeant Harris just made a very nice collar, that's what.'

'Eh?'

'You remember those "no visible trace of entry" jobs?'

Houston's heart sank.

'Yes?'

'Got 'em bang to rights. Two blokes – with a girl helping 'em – only a kid, in care as a matter of fact.'

Benson swirled hot water round the pot.

'Funny thing was, we were all right about those jobs.'

'How?'

'Well, the two of 'em came from outside the manor, as we said.'

'Oh,' grunted Houston.

'But you were right as well. They were making kids help 'em, you know, leaving doors and windows open at night. Threatening 'em with violence.'

'Grange Hill kids?'

'Some of 'em,' agreed Benson.

Houston smirked: 'How did Sergeant Harris get 'em? Did he go to the school?'

Benson looked at Houston, then grinned.

'Oh no. The school came to us. In a way, you might say the school made the collar. Have a cup, Brian.'

Houston drank. Harris was right. Benson did make a good cup of tea.

' 'Course, I know it's not your favourite tipple,' added Benson slyly.

'Eh, what's that?'

'I hear you were drinking with Garfield the Grange Hill caretaker the other night.'

'Oh him,' Houston cleared his throat. 'Well we did have a little chat. I think it's worth while.' He put his cup down on the desk.

'I reckon there's something peculiar going on at that school.'

He was right of course. But just how peculiar, he had no idea. Doyle was about to put Plan C into operation.

Chapter 29

Tucker had arrived at the school gate late as usual, but just in time for the aggro over Cathy Hargreaves. !n fact he'd got there just as Bullet Baxter thumped the big kid. In fairness to Baxter he had to admit that the other bloke had hit Baxter first. But Baxter had done more damage and afterwards they'd carried the bloke away in a police car. Maybe he should put one on Doyle, like that.

But Tucker had it the wrong way round. It was Doyle who was about to put one on him. In the classroom there was a good deal of muttering going on, but no one seemed to be talking to Tucker. That was suspicious. At break time he began to get the drift. They were talking about the Semolina Sensation, the Sponsored Run as the joker had called it. Tucker chuckled. After all, the twits should never have started it. Eating flipping semolina all week! Slurp-in! Big kids!

But now the talk was all about how it happened. 'Who sponsored the runs?' as one kid put it.

'Could be anybody,' offered Tucker.

'No, it couldn't,' said Benny.

'Why not?'

'Because about sixty of us copped it, that's what. It couldn't be them, could it? It could only be somebody who wasn't in the semo thing.'

'Or somebody who was taking the mickey,' Doyle suddenly interrupted, looking straight at Tucker.

'What are you getting at, Doyle?' Tucker made a threatening move and Doyle's heavies moved in. Tucker cooled it because he remembered Macker owed him one for the pounding he gave him in class last week.

'I'm not getting at anyone,' said Doyle. 'But if they start investigating, there'll be trouble. If the boss finds out someone did put the stuff in the semo, then their feet won't touch the ground.'

'Who says anybody put stuff in?' said Tucker. 'Could be a bug.'

'Yeah, and pigs might fly,' answered Doyle. 'Someone was messing about. Thought it was a giggle, making people sick.'

'My heart bleeds and I bet yours does, too,' said Tucker. Macker lunged at him. Tucker suddenly realized he was on his own. He remembered some of his own mates had been on the Semolina Run and he'd laughed. That was stupid. Hey – if they thought . . . He turned and moved off in search of his friends. But there was no sign of them in the yard. And he got no chance to talk to them in class. What a life. As soon as one thing was put right, another went wrong.

What Tucker didn't know was how wrong.

After last period, a lad came to him by the cloaks.

'Jenkins. You're wanted urgently at the staffroom. Mr Sutcliffe.'

Grumbling, Tucker grabbed his bag and went round to the staffroom. But he never reached it. As he turned the corner he was seized and frog-marched down the corridor, then pushed against the staffroom wall. It was Doyle and his crowd. Who else?

'It was you who got me here, was it, Doyle?'

'Shut up, Jenkins.' Doyle raised his voice to a shout.

'Listen, Jenkins, you rat. Everybody in school knows you put stuff in that semolina. Own up, you rat.'

'You — ,' swore Tucker.

'Own up, own up,' they chanted.

The staffroom door flew open. They scattered and ran. Tucker ran too, but not before he saw Baxter standing in the corridor, glaring at him.

Chapter 30

Tucker ran until he was outside the school gates. Doyle and Co. had vanished But where were his mates, when he needed them? Nowhere. He stood for a second on the pavement looking left and right. No sign. And freezing cold, too. He buttoned his jacket and wished he'd brought his anorak this morning. The bus came charging down the main street and Tucker ran for it. Too late. The driver saw him coming and got clean away, leaving him grabbing for empty air.

No use waiting. He crossed the road and dawdled along by the shops. The windows were full of gift-wrapped packages – the same old rubbish they'd had all year tarted up for Christmas. Even the thought of less than two weeks to go to the holiday didn't help. Things had turned bad. Doyle had hung him out. And this last caper could be really dodgy. He'd have to have a word with the lads. But where were they?

'First sign of old age, Tucker. Talking to yourself.'

He looked up. Surrounding him were four girls, Pongo Yates, the Lewis person and another couple. They all looked alike to him. He tried to push past but they blocked his way.

'Can we have a word with you, Peter?' said Penny Lewis in her posh voice.

'Come on, Tucker,' said the third girl. 'Come and have a coffee. We won't eat you.'

He thought gloomily, They're murder when they gang up on you. He shrugged.

'OK, but you lot pay.'

'But of course, Tucker,' said Trisha.

They took his arm and steered him into the café. That was the second time he'd been taken prisoner and he had a suspicion this was all to do with the same business. He was right.

When they had sat down with the coffees, Trisha said:

'Did you put stuff in the semolina?'

He jumped up: 'Get lost!' he said and started for the door. The fourth girl put her leg out and tripped him up. The other helped him back to the table.

'Don't go, please, Peter,' said Penny.

Trisha asked: 'Tucker. Did you?'

'No.'

'There you are.' She turned to Penny. 'That's 50p you owe me. I said it wasn't his style.' Then she spoiled it by adding, 'I mean he's stupid, but not sneaky.'

They all grinned at him. He drank his coffee.

'Question is,' said Penny, 'who?'

'Doyle,' said Tucker.

'You would say that.'

'It'd fit,' said the third girl. 'He's been trying to put something on Tucker all week. This afternoon he was spreading it round that Tucker was the poisoner and ought to be forced to own up.'

'Oh yes,' said Trisha. 'Tucker made him put back that pistol he knocked off from the Art Department that time. This might be revenge.'

'How d'you prove it?'

'I'll soon prove it,' said Tucker.

'Nobody'll believe you,' said Trisha.

'If we knew how it was done,' said Penny. 'I mean how could anybody have got into the kitchen and put it in the pot?'

'Besides,' said the third girl, 'why didn't everybody get the whatsits?'

'Hey, that's right,' said Trisha. 'I didn't.'

'We noticed,' said the girl, eyeing Trisha.

Trisha looked down at the table.

'Hey, what about that?'

'What?'

'The sugar. I don't take it. I didn't have any on my semo.'

'I did.'

'And me.'

'Brown sugar,' said Trisha. 'Suppose somebody mixed laxative in with the brown sugar.'

'How could they?' said Tucker. 'It's either chocolate stuff or senna pods, isn't it?'

'No,' said Penny, 'the Health Shop.'

'The which?'

'The Health Shop at the end here. Lots of stuff there. Laxative powders, natural, gentle, quick-acting.'

'What are we waiting for?' asked Trisha.

Chapter 31

Michael Doyle was at ease with the world, modestly proud of the success of his plans A, B and C. If only he could tell his dad. The old man would be proud of him. He sat in the dining-hall lingering over his rice pudding. His side-kicks had left already. He stayed on to think about his next move. Just how to close the trap he had placed around Jenkins. The thought gave him great pleasure.

Suddenly he realized he was not alone. Seated in a row across the table were the strangest assortment of people – Penny Lewis, Trisha Yates, Cathy Hargreaves – what next? – Tucker Jenkins, Benny Green, Alan Humphries. They watched him carefully as he raised his spoon.

'Enjoying your pudding, Michael?' asked Trisha.

He stared at her.

'Is it sweet enough?'

'Yes, thank you.'

'Are you sure?' She reached over to the table behind her and suddenly put a big bowl in front of him. Taking a spoon she quickly spread two big spoonfuls of brown crystals over his pudding.

'Hey, get off!' said Doyle.

'Eat it up, Michael. It's only brown sugar. I thought you had a sweet tooth.'

'How do I know it's brown sugar?'

'What else could it be?' asked Penny. 'Laxative powder mixed with brown sugar, perhaps?'

'No,' said Tucker. 'Couldn't be. I mean, who'd play a rotten trick like that?'

'That's right, Michael, dear,' said Trisha. 'Eat up your pud like a good little boy.'

'Tell you what,' said Cathy. 'Let's fetch Matron. She may be worried. This sudden loss of appetite.'

Doyle stood up, but Tucker leaned over and pushed him down.

Trisha said: 'Listen, Doyle, you rat. Either you eat that now or we're going to Mr Llewellyn and we're going to tell him you put that stuff in the semolina and why you did it.'

Doyle blustered. 'You're guessing. There's no proof.'

'Oh, there is, Michael,' said Penny. 'The lady in the Health Shop remembers you. She said you were the first boy she'd ever seen buying laxative.'

'Eat up, man,' said Benny Green. 'It's getting cold.'

Doyle gulped, then began to eat in great mouthfuls, pushing the pudding down his throat as quickly as possible. When he'd finished he leapt up from the table and ran from the dining-hall. They watched him go.

Penny said: 'Rough justice, Trisha.'

'Get away with you,' answered Trisha. 'There was nothing on that pudding but brown sugar and bicarbonate of soda. His imagination's done the rest.'

Chapter 32

Justin was half way down Kettlewell Street when the car drew up alongside him. His mother looked out of the window.

'I was just along here talking to some parents about tonight's meeting, when I saw you, Justin. I'll give you a lift home.'

He hesitated, saw her expression and climbed in beside her. She started the car again and then turned to him.

'I shouldn't really tell you fibs, Justin. I followed you along. I wanted to know what you were up to. I mean what you have been up to for ages now.'

He did not answer. She shrugged.

'All right, dear. Let's just go home and have a cup of tea. Then, I want to know. I think I've waited long enough for you to tell me of your own accord, and covered up for you with your father as well.'

Justin turned red. They drove on in silence until they reached home. Then both of them went into the kitchen. While his mother put the kettle on, Justin slowly unpacked the scrapbook and spread it out on the kitchen table. His mother stood with the tea-pot watching as he turned the pages and explained, until the kettle shrieked.

'Justin, why the secrecy?'

'I don't know, Mum, really. Except that I was sure Dad would think it all a waste of time. I mean there's not much, is there?'

'Justin, I think it's fantastic. I bet nobody has told

the story of this area in this way before. It makes you feel part of it, somehow . . .'

'That's it, Mum. We move around so much. Dad's work and all. I wanted to belong with something.'

She poured out the tea.

'Why do you think I'm so keen on this parents' thing, Justin?'

He sipped his tea then said, hesitantly:

'It won't be much good, if I have to change school, will it?'

'Oh, you're an ass, Justin. If your father had known what you were up to he'd never have bothered about you changing school. He just thinks you've been messing about. I mean, sometimes you do rather.'

'Sometimes I think I won't ever catch up with what Dad wants.'

'Justin!' His mother looked at him, then turned away.

'Listen. I am sure we can get your father to agree you stay at Grange Hill. He'll be in later. Don't say anything to him until I get back from the parents' meeting and then we'll both have a go at him.'

'Thanks, Mum.'

'Don't be silly. And don't be so secretive.'

'Mum. I shall have to go back and see to Mrs Carter's place – the cat and all.'

'Do you want a lift, Justin? I'll be driving down to the meeting.'

'Thanks, Mum, drop me off at the top of Kettlewell, will you?'

'Right. Let's have tea now, Justin, I'm famished.'

Chapter 33

While Mrs Bennett got ready for the parents' meeting, another candidate for the elections was having a spot of
bother. Benny got home to find a big row going on. Well,
his dad wasn't talking much, but Mrs Green was. He sat
in the armchair. She stood, coat and hat on, arms on hips,
by the door.

'Get it straight, Sam Green. You're going to no meeting.
The state your back's in after all that chasing those boys,
you've got to rest it. Otherwise you'll not be fit to start
that job on Monday.'

Sam Green exploded.

'Woman, don't you understand? If I don't get to the
meeting, who's going to vote for me? If I don't get elected,
then that man Robinson gets in.'

'Don't you "woman" me. You know my name. If you
don't get elected it isn't the end of the world.'

Sam half rose in his chair.

'I'm going and you're not stopping me.'

Mrs Green opened her handbag. 'You're going nowhere.
See what I've got here, your car keys. And you don't
try and start it like Peter Jenkins started that dumper
truck.'

She saw Benny.

'Benjamin Green, your tea is on the table. You do the
washing up. I'll see you both at ten o'clock.'

Out she went, leaving Benny and his dad looking at
each other. Benny got on with his tea and Sam Green
picked up his newspaper.

There was a knock on the back door. Tucker looked in.

'Benny. They're all off to the meeting. What say we . . .'

He stopped short. 'Oh, hello, Mr Green. Thought you were . . .'

Benny shook his head. 'Ma took the car keys – Dad can't go.'

'Hey, that's crazy. How's he going to get elected?'

The two Greens looked at him in silence.

'Do we know someone who can give you a lift?' went on Tucker.

Sam Green shook his head.

'Tell you what. I've got my old truck in the garage.'

'Dah, talk sense, Tucker,' said Benny.

Tucker wasn't giving up: 'Old Mrs Carter, down Kettlewell. She's got a wheelchair. She'd give us a lend of it. How about that, Mr Green? You know her.'

A devilish gleam came into Sam Green's eye.

'She just might, Tucker, boy. She just might.'

Five minutes later Tucker and Benny were ringing and hammering on Mrs Carter's door. There was no answer. They looked at one another.

'She must be asleep, or away or something.'

'Well, that means no wheelchair,' said Benny.

'Get off. Have a look below. There's a little place under these stairs.' Tucker led the way. But the door under the stairs was padlocked. He kicked the wall in frustration.

'Pound to a peanut she keeps it here. Hey, Benny, run home and get a screw-driver.'

Benny turned towards the pavement, then stopped.

'Hey, Justin, what are you doing here?'

Justin, who stood on the pavement a few feet away,

watching them, said:

'I know what I'm doing here. I'm checking things are all right for Mrs Carter. But what are you two doing?'

'Hey, Justin,' said Tucker, 'does that mean you've got the keys. Come on. We want the wheelchair.'

Justin came closer. 'You're crazy. You can't pinch Mrs Carter's wheelchair. What are you up to?'

Tucker said, threateningly: 'How are you going to stop us?'

Justin stood his ground.

'I don't know, but I am.'

'Look, Tucker. That's no way to talk,' interrupted Benny. Turning to Justin, he rapidly explained the situation. He added:

'Mrs Carter'd lend it to my dad, for sure.'

Justin looked doubtful. Benny pressed his point.

'Justin. Your ma – she's going to get elected. So you're all right, eh? But what about my dad? What about his chance?'

Justin hesitated a second, then:

'OK,' he said. 'But I'm coming with you. I'm not having that wheelchair damaged.'

'Right on, Justin,' said Benny.

Five minutes later the three lads with the wheelchair passed down Kettlewell. Another ten minutes after that, they reappeared at a trot with an embarrassed Sam Green clinging on to the chair-arms. As they passed, Det-con. Houston, waiting in his observation post, stared, rubbed his eyes, then let in the clutch and gently followed.

At the same time, in Grange Hill Police Station, the phone rang. Sergeant Harris answered it, listened with raised eyebrows, then drew pad and pen towards him.

Then he turned and called: 'Alf! Message from a lady

111

in Kettlewell Street. West Indian gentleman in stolen wheelchair, with three boys, proceeding east.'

He put down the phone.

'Switch the kettle off and get the car out. This could be fun.'

Chapter 34

Fun was not Sam Green's word for it. Before they had got to the end of Kettlewell Street and turned towards the shopping centre, he had begun to regret it. The old wheelchair ran smoothly enough, but the three lads pushing it had different ideas about how and how fast. Justin was more skilled, the other two were stronger. First the pressure one side was heavier, then on the other, and the wheelchair zigzagged wildly about the pavement, with Justin trying desperately to prevent it from scraping on walls or running into the road. As they reached one junction and were poised to cross the road, Sam spoke at last.

'You boys. Can't you push in turns? I can't stand it with three drivers.'

'Dead right, Mr Green,' shouted Tucker. 'I'll go first. Stand back,' he called to the other two and launched Mr Green full tilt into the road as a car slammed on its brakes and a white-faced driver looked out at them.

Sam Green raised his hand.

'Sorry, ma'am.'

'Just running in,' pleaded Tucker.

The driver shook her head, waved them over and drove on. Behind them, Det-con. Houston thought quickly whether to stop and take a note of what had happened, then decided not to risk losing them, and pressed on at their rear.

As they trundled to the end of the road, Benny, who had

turned round to check the next crossing, said:

'Hey, fellers. Trouble. Flash Harry's following us.'

'Justin,' commanded Tucker. 'Come on this side. Let's get a bit of speed on.'

The chair shot forward. Sam Green gritted his teeth. They took the next corner on one wheel.

'He's still there,' called Benny.

'Right wheel!' yelled Tucker, and swung the wheel-chair up the slope and into the park. 'Come on, Benny. Give's a push, up the hill.'

A frustrated Det-con. Houston saw the three vanish into the park. Perhaps they were just taking the bloke for a walk. Still, a queer old walk. At that speed they were going to do him a mischief. He drove on and took the car round in the direction of the main road.

Meanwhile, the three charioteers struggled up the hill in the park. The slope was short, but steep, and Sam Green was no light weight.

'Don't let it roll back,' shouted Tucker. 'All push together now.'

They did. The chair took the rise like a Rolls-Royce and went over the top.

'Hey,' Tucker gasped, 'stop pushing!'

'We're not,' answered the others. The chair had taken charge and they were being dragged, tripping and stumbling, down the slope towards the park gates on the other side. Tucker fell and let go, Benny's legs were swept from under him. Now the chair was running free, and Mr Green, his forehead starting with perspiration, was hauling back on the sidewheels in a huge effort to stop the chair, which was now bowling down the hill out of control.

Justin never knew whether he was thinking of chair or

114

passenger, but he staggered to his feet, left the other two, sprinted in front of the chair, put out both hands, fell, slid under it like John Wayne doing his stage coach act, caught the axle and, sliding and bumping along the ground, halted it.

They came in a great sliding rush, all four of them together, to the zebra on the main road, just as Det-con. Houston, who had circled round, came driving up. He barely had time to brake, before they were crossing the road almost under his bumpers, Mr Green saluting him courteously.

'Hey, Justin,' said Benny anxiously, 'your clothes, and your face. You've got a black eye.'

'Come on,' said Tucker. 'We're late already.'

Mr Garfield was coming from his cubby hole, one eye on the clock and wondering how long the parents' meeting would last and if he could get the place locked up by ten o'clock, when he saw something that made him rub his eyes and look again.

He thought he saw three lads pushing a wheelchair with a man in it across the hall.

'Hey,' he called uncertainly. But when he reached the corridor into the hall, they had vanished. He went back to his cubby hole shaking his head.

The famous four wheeled smartly down the corridor and full tilt through the swing doors into the Assembly Hall. Then just as suddenly, they reversed and shot back out again, before Mr Llewellyn, Councillor Doyle and the other worthies on the platform could see what had happened.

For in the middle of the hall, crowded with parents, a lady was on her feet, hand raised, voice ringing out.

115

'And if Mr Robinson thinks we're going to accept this nonsense he has another think coming.'

It was Mrs Green.

'Lads,' said her husband. 'Let's get out of here, fast.'

Chapter 35

The wheelchair party was in full flight down the corridor, when Benny whispered:

'Hey, do you think anybody saw us?'

'Nah,' said Tucker. 'Look, one big heave and straight out through the front doors.'

But they came into the hall just as Garfield made another sortie from his cubby hole. Without thinking, they swung right, down a side passage.

Garfield saw them this time.

'Hey, you there!'

But they were gone again, down the corridor. This time Garfield was following.

'Quick, into this side room,' urged Tucker.

They heard the caretaker crash past, reversed the chair and shot out again, U-turned and headed down the corridor, just as Garfield reached the door at the other end. He caught a glimpse of them as they took the corner and doubled back. But he was way behind.

For the second time they made the run up to the main doors. Benny ran in front, pulled them open, and with Justin and Tucker in perfect control, they went out like a cork from a bottle.

Just as Det-con. Houston, headlights blazing, swung his old car into the school drive.

'To your right,' said Tucker hoarsely. The wheelchair swung across the concrete, over the grass and in among the laurel bushes, now dank and musty in the dark of the winter evening.

Det-con. Houston, stopping his car and getting out, missed this manoeuvre, but he did see a shadowy figure leave the main doors and run into the bushes to the right.

As he slammed the car door shut, another car drew up behind him. To his disgust he saw Sergeant Harris and PC Benson.

'I'm going to cut 'em off,' he called and raced away into the shrubbery.

Sergeant Harris watched him go with a shake of the head.

'That could be painful for somebody,' he said. 'Come on, Alf, let's just go inside and have a word with the caretaker or someone.'

There was no sign of the caretaker, but the corridor was full of parents streaming out from the meeting. Mr Llewellyn spotted the police and hurried forward to meet them, frowning.

'Well, Sergeant?'

Harris suddenly felt embarrassed.

'I don't know quite how to put this, Mr Llewellyn. But did anyone see three boys with a black gentleman in a wheelchair come into the school? A stolen wheelchair,' he added hastily.

Mr Llewellyn looked at the sergeant, thoughtfully.

'No, Sergeant, I think that if we'd seen them, it would have registered.'

'Someone was seen in the grounds, sir. Might we have a look?'

'I'll come with you myself, Sergeant,' said the Head.

The three men walked quickly from the school and looked around them in the cold darkness.

'This way, I think, sir,' said Benson, pointing to where

he had seen Houston disappear.

'Lead on, Alf,' answered Sergeant Harris.

From behind their laurel bush, the wheelchair party watched them go.

'Quick,' whispered Tucker. 'Before people come out for their cars.'

They swung the chair back on to the drive and were away swiftly and smoothly before the first parents reached the door.

Mr Llewellyn with his police escort rounded the bushes and flower beds and came on to the open grass patch beyond. There they stopped and stared.

'Mr Garfield,' said the Head, in a shocked voice.

The caretaker, fists doubled, hair over his eyes and his shirt ripped open, stood aggressively over a body on the ground.

Looking up at them, one hand clutching the torn neck of Mr Garfield's shirt, was Det-con. Houston.

Sergeant Harris looked down at him with compassion. Then he grinned.

'Why, Brian. You've got a collar at last.'

Mrs Bennett ran her car into the garage, locked it and walked quickly into the house.

'Hello you two,' she called.

Her husband answered. 'Hello, dear. We're in the study.'

She pushed open the door, talking as she went.

'Well, the meeting was a complete success. Mr Green and I are both on the committee, thanks, I'd say, to an absolutely fantastic speech by Mrs Green.'

She stopped and looked at her husband.

'What's wrong, dear?'

He said nothing but pointed to an armchair where her son sat.

'Hello, Mum,' he said miserably.

'Justin. What have you done to your face, and your clothes?'

'I don't know how to tell you, Mum,' he answered.

Chapter 36

Next morning there was an emergency Year Assembly. On the platform, Miss Peterson spoke briefly.

'First the good news. Mr Sutcliffe reports a splendid entry for his competition – some first rate stories and poems and a magnificent project. No names, yet.'

She paused and looked round.

'I don't need to tell you the bad news, with our sponsorship projects. As well as the semolina people did before their project was suspended, we still cannot raise enough to beat Brookdale. Unless, of course, we have a last minute mass entry for the Sponsored Walk. So, I'm appealing to you . . .'

She stopped as the Headmaster's secretary came to the platform and handed her a note.

'Oh,' she said. 'Jenkins and Green. To the Head's office, at the double.'

Tucker and Benny got to their feet and looked at one another.

'After you,' said Benny.

Their worst fears were made real as they entered the office. There sat Llewellyn, his face like stone. On a chair at the side of his desk, sat a tall man in rimless glasses. A little farther away, his face still bruised and marked, sat Justin.

Benny and Tucker lined up. They weren't invited to sit down.

'Jenkins. This is that moment I was afraid would arrive before term end. But I'm compelled to hear your side of it, whatever my feelings on the matter. Last night there was an incident which brought the police to the school and resulted in injury to one of them.'

Tucker and Benny looked at one another, eyes wide.

'There are good reasons to believe that Bennett, Green and you, Jenkins, were involved. Bennett, however, for reasons of loyalty which I feel are probably wasted in this case, has refused to say anything, beyond saying that he takes his share of any responsibility.

'Since I cannot punish without real evidence I am relying upon you to tell me what happened. Otherwise the main burden will fall upon Bennett. His parents, I might say, are inclined to take him away from the school. So Jenkins, what do you have to say? Let me tell you right away, I am interested only in the truth.'

Tucker looked at Justin, then at Benny, then cleared his throat.

'Sir, you're not going to believe . . .'

'Just tell us, Jenkins.'

Tucker began to explain. He told the story carefully from beginning to end. It was ridiculous. Even if he'd thought it was worth it, he couldn't have invented anything more fantastic. He didn't even believe it himself. But he knew it had happened, so he went on telling it.

The Head's face was expressionless. From the corner of his eyes he could see a cynical smile on the face of the man with glasses – who must be Mr Bennett. That put him off, but he ploughed on and finished his piece.

'Is that all, Jenkins? What about you, Green?'

Benny shook his head. Mr Llewellyn turned to Justin's father.

'Well, Mr Bennett?'

Justin's father answered coldly.

'Headmaster, I don't believe a word of it. Just a small

matter of credibility. Mrs Bennett and some 150 other people, including yourself, were there in the school. And three boys, a wheelchair and a grown man were crashing in and out of the place during the meeting without being seen?'

The Head sighed. 'I did warn you, Jenkins. Now . . .'

'Sir, it's the truth.' Tucker was desperate.

'Jenkins,' Mr Llewellyn raised his voice.

'Excuse me, Headmaster.'

'Yes, Mr Bennett?'

'I said I didn't believe it. But I'm full of admiration.'

'I'm not quite with you, Mr Bennett.'

Justin's father looked at Tucker and suddenly grinned. 'It's the most fantastic piece of invention I've ever heard. It's helped me make up my mind about whether Justin should change schools.'

'And?'

'I'd like him to stay. If, when I was at school, I'd had friends who were prepared to put themselves into real trouble, to invent such incredible stories just to get their pal off the hook, then I'd have enjoyed life a great deal more than I did. I think Justin's very lucky and I was mistaken in thinking he should leave.'

The Head was speechless for a moment.

'Very well, Mr Bennett.'

Justin's father rose: 'If you'll excuse me, I must go. I appreciate all your trouble, Headmaster. As far as I'm concerned I hope that this business can be allowed to blow over. But after all, that's your decision. However, I'd like Justin to stay.'

He left the room. Tucker burst out:

'Sir. I was telling the truth.'

The Head looked at him helplessly.

'Jenkins, I have to believe you. But if that is the truth,

what would an invented story be like?'

'Sir,' asked Justin. 'Is the – policeman all right?'

Mr Llewellyn raised his eyebrows. 'I'm assured by the sergeant, that on their part they have no complaints and do not wish to pursue the matter. I think that on my part I would find it less complicated to close the question myself.'

Outside the Head's office, Tucker said:

'Come on, let's get back.'

'Back where?'

'To the assembly, dimbo.'

'What for?'

'I've just had a fantastic idea for a sponsored event.'

'Get off.'

'I have. Want to hear it?'

'OK.'

'Well, come on then!'

Want to hear it? Well read on then. Next page, dimbo!

For those who are interested, Grange Hill won the fund-raising contest with Brookdale, thanks to an incredible Wheelchair, Pram and Pushchair Marathon run by the school – an idea suggested by guess who?

Justin Bennett's 'Memory Scrapbook' won the competition and was displayed in the Library. You may have seen Mrs Carter on the box. She's quite a celebrity now.

Tucker entered his poem for the competition. It didn't win a prize, but Tucker has allowed us to publish the last two verses.

GRANGE HILL

There's no place like Grange Hill
    I bet you,
'Cos if you bunk off – they
    won't let you,
And if you stay, they come
    and get you.
The place is like a prison,
    there's no doubt.
But if they really want to punish you, they
    throw you out.

Grange Hill, Grange Hill, I love you so,
I'll have my ashes scattered when I go.
And as I fall in little gritty bits,
I'll see Llewellyn having fifty fits.
He'll say, that's just like Jenkins, messy pup,
So, Mr Garfield come and sweep him up.

The Third Class Genie

ROBERT LEESON

Disasters were leading two nil on Alec's disaster-triumph scorecard, when he slipped into the vacant factory lot, locally known as the Tank. Ginger Wallace was hot on his heels, ready to destroy him, and Alec had escaped just in the nick of time. There were disasters awaiting him at home too, when he discovered that he would have to move out of his room and into the boxroom. And, of course, there was school . . .

But Alec's luck changed when he found a beer can that was still sealed, but obviously empty. Stranger still, when he held it up to his ear, he could hear a faint snoring . . . When Alec finally opened the mysterious can, something happened that gave triumphs a roaring and most unexpected lead.

A hilarious story for readers of ten upwards.

Nobody's Family Is Going To Change

LOUISE FITZHUGH

Emma Sheridan is an intelligent black 11-year-old, a compulsive eater, determined to become a distinguished lawyer. Her father is a lawyer himself, but the last thing in the world he can imagine is his daughter – a *female* – addressing the court.

Emma's brother, Willie, has one overriding dream; to be a dancer like his Uncle Dipsey. But Willie's parents, who want Willie to be the lawyer, don't think dancing is what their son should be doing.

Is there something wrong with them, Emma wonders? Or is there something wrong with their parents, who won't accept any reversal of traditional roles?

In her rebellion against parental prejudices, Emma learns much about herself and others.

Children's Rights Workshop awarded this book their Other Award for the best children's novel of 1976. 'Underlying the comedy, Louise Fitzhugh reveals a sympathy for children and an understanding of their struggles that make this book a landmark in writing for young people.'

'Miss Fitzhugh's observation of children's feelings and doings is wonderfully exact. More than that it is wonderfully funny.' *The Times*

Harriet the Spy

LOUISE FITZHUGH

Harriet the Spy has a secret notebook which she fills with utterly honest jottings about her parents, her friends and her neighbours. This, she feels sure, will prepare her for her career as a famous writer. Every day on her spy route, she scrutinizes, observes and notes down anything of interest to her:

Laura Peters is thinner and uglier. I think she could do with some braces on her teeth.

Once I thought I wanted to be Franca. But she's so dull if I was her I couldn't stand myself, I guess it's not money that makes people dull. I better find out because I might be it.

If Marion Hawthorne doesn't watch out she's going to grow up into a lady Hitler.

But Harriet commits the unforgivable for a spy – she is unmasked. When her notebook is found by her school friends, their anger and retaliation and Harriet's unexpected responses explode in an hilarious and often touching way.

'Harriet M. Welsch is one of the meatiest heroines in modern juvenile literature. This novel is a *tour de force*.'

Library Journal

'This devastatingly shrewd, ruefully comic picture of the young makes a good many characters in children's fiction seem like wet dish-cloths.'

Sunday Times